Praise for Loren D. Estleman and SWEET WOMEN LIE

"Mr. Estleman turns in a tight, well-oiled plot and some catchy characterizations."
The New York Times Book Review

"Amos Walker is the best tough guy detective in the country. He brushes against the darkest corners of Detroit but he shines them up as he passes."
Detroit Free Press

"The Walker books are among the most enjoyable being written today in the classic private eye field . . . impressively crafted, at once sentimental and cynical."
San Francisco Examiner

"Estleman is remarkably true to Chandler's hard-boiled form without parodying it, and Walker remains today's most moral and loyal private eye."
The Orlando Sentinel

SWEET WOMEN LIE

Loren D. Estleman

FAWCETT CREST · NEW YORK

A Fawcett Crest Book
Published by Ballantine Books
Copyright © 1990 by Loren D. Estleman

Library of Congress Catalog Card Number: 89-49640

ISBN 0-449-21944-5

First published by Houghton Mifflin Company. Reprinted by permission of Houghton Mifflin Company.

Manufactured in the United States of America

First Ballantine Books Edition: February 1992

This is the one Helen and Don have been waiting for.

1

THE CLUB CANAVERAL'S RAINBOW FRONT DIED SHORT OF
the alley that ran alongside the building. Not for me the side
that faced Griswold, where orange flamingos capered in the
windows and a pink neon tube—turned off by daylight—
scripted over a particolored awning that when cranked up
resembled a roll of Life Savers. I stood in the alley among
caved-in trash cans and smears of pale disinfectant powder
flung over places where patrons had lost supper, pushed a
button next to a brown steel fire door without a handle, and
listened to the brazen noise inside. It sounded like a tired
musician clearing his spit valve.

She surprised me by opening the door herself. I had been
expecting the janitor, or at most one of the abbed and latted
specimens in white disco suits who posed with her in newspaper advertisements. If I *had* been expecting her, it would
have been in five-inch heels and piles of yellow hair and a
dress that pushed her white breasts up through the hole in
the ozone. It wouldn't have had anything to do with this small
slim woman wearing flat heels and a man's denim workshirt
with the tail out over black jeans. She wore her hair in a
ponytail, brown, not blond, with silver glittering in the part.
Her face was creased lightly around the eyes and at the corners of the wide handsome mouth that the caricaturists had
had so much fun with when she dated Frankie Avalon. She

1

looked a well-scrubbed, well-exercised forty, which put her a couple of years past her studio biography. Well, the white-haired moguls decomposing in their big oak cigar-smelling offices back then knew the teen audience, or thought they did. And what they thought was what we got.

I said, "You looked taller in my bedroom."

It didn't throw her. The wide mouth measured out forty watts of the famous thousand-candlepower smile. "Which poster was it, *Beach Blowout* or *V-8 Vampires*?"

"*Vampires*. You had on a shiny black leather jumpsuit unzipped to China. It ruined me for all the girls in the eleventh grade."

"Don't tell me. You had a surfboard and a stop sign on the other walls."

"Just the poster. I was too straight a kid to steal signs and there's no surf in Michigan. I'm Amos Walker." I took off my hat. Grainy November snow slid out of the dent.

"Gail Hope. But I guess you know that." She gave me the loan of a small supple palm. "Come inside."

We were at the end of a shallow hallway lined with framed publicity stills from Gail Hope's pictures. These included a honey of a shot of Miss Hope in a white sharkskin swimsuit fainting in the scabrous arms of a creature that appeared to be half reptile and half diseased elm. The rest-room doors were divided into sexes by cutouts of Marilyn Monroe and James Dean pasted on them. She led me, trim white ankles scissoring under the barrel cuffs of her jeans, across the nightclub proper, dimly lit by sunlight through partially drawn blinds, to a door marked OFFICE. On the way we passed a lot of tulip-shaped tables and Brando biker posters and a divan made from the rear end of a 1960 Cadillac with tailfins. The walls were sea-green and pale orange, the floor a checkerboard of charcoal and pink. Evenings the colored lights played off paper lanterns, and musicians got up like Bobby Rydell and Connie Francis performed doo-wop on a bandstand the size of Warren Beatty's wallet. By day it all seemed kind of tired, like a trick-or-treater on November first, but at night you could sit back sipping from a glass with an umbrella in it and pretend that John, Paul, George, and Ringo were still planning the invasion and Caroline and John-John were playing on the White House lawn.

The office had none of that. The desk was black-painted steel with a Formica top like the ones that migrate to gas stations, with a swivel behind it and a blank-faced computer on a stand. An Impressionist painting of a city street hung on the back wall in lieu of a window and there were only two photographs. One, in a clear Lucite stand on the desk, looked like a nonprofessional shot of Gail Hope taken twenty years ago. The other, on the wall, was definitely a much younger Miss Hope sitting on a sofa and sharing a laugh with a sandy-haired young man in an open-necked shirt and baggy plaid sportcoat. It took a moment to recognize him as Elvis before the black dye job and white Vegas gravity suit. She couldn't have been more than fourteen.

She saw me looking at the girl on the desk. "My daughter Evelyn. She's studying law at UCLA."

"I guess you didn't want her in show business."

"Her choice. I'm glad she made it. At least this way if she winds up on drugs it won't be because a studio doctor made her take them." She took my hat and coat and hung them on an antique halltree, the oldest thing in the building. She frowned approvingly at what the coat had been covering. We sat. I watched her fish a pack of Bel-Airs and a book of matches out of the top drawer.

"I own the building, I pay the taxes," she said, lighting up. "If you're worried about black lung, you know where the door is."

I grinned and borrowed her matches to light a Winston.

Relaxing a little, she sat back, planted an elbow on the arm of her swivel, and pointed her cigarette at the ceiling. "Just to dispel any pesky illusions: I wasn't a virgin when they cast me in my first beach picture and the only reason I agreed to do it was the studio promised me the whore in an Edward Albee play and they wanted a two-picture deal. Then they scrapped the Albee and gave me a biker show instead. After that I was typecast. My leading man in *Beach Blowout*

3

was living with a Beverly Hills men's-room attendant and every time the director said cut, the old-fart star from Hollywood's Golden Age they cast as my father stuck his big sweaty hand inside my bikini. Disappointed?''

"Devastated. I feel like going straight home and smashing my forty-five of 'Johnny Jump-Up.' ''

Her quick little smile sharpened the creases at the corners of her mouth. They could almost be passed off as dimples. "It isn't even my voice on the record. It wasn't enough to be the season's biggest drive-in draw, you had to be a recording star too. My agent's idea, the old souse. I stopped sleeping with him soon after and he cut his wrists like a hysterical old woman. The studio could have hired Hitchcock for what it cost them to hush it up. See, I'm nobody's Gidget.''

"You're as tough as old gravy, all right.''

"You say that now, but would you have gone back to see me seven times if you knew the truth then?''

"I never saw any of your pictures even once.''

That opened her eyes a notch. They looked different without the thick fringed lashes. "You have a *V-8 Vampires* poster in your room and you didn't go to see it?''

"There wasn't any money in my house for movies. When yours got to TV I was working nights. My father worked in a steel foundry when they weren't paying much.''

"You were lucky. Mine cut out when I was seven. When I was making thirty-five hundred a week he came back and took me to court. They made me pay for his support.'' She blew a dagger of smoke and crushed out her cigarette in a plain glass ashtray that was probably a collector's item in some circles. "I got your name from L. C. Candy. He gave you information on some old jazzman you were looking for. You made a good impression.''

"I remember him. Did he play here?''

"Who, Candy? I couldn't use him. There were no trombones in the early sixties. I rented him a room upstairs cheap while he was looking. He got a steady playing backup at the Chord Progression finally. I hear from him now and then. You ever carry money for anyone?''

4

"I'm bonded."

"That's not what I asked."

"Sometimes. It's not my specialty. Who's shaking you down?"

She made a sound that was supposed to pass for laughter. It didn't resemble her Malibu giggle. "If you knew as much about my private life as the slugs who used to read *Rendezvous*, you'd know how funny that one is."

"Sam Lucy," I said.

"Maybe you did read *Rendezvous*."

"Call it osmosis." Gail Hope and Samuel Frederick Lucy—pinball, restaurants, cleaning and dyeing, and any other business that dealt largely in cash that could be exchanged for money skimmed off the tables in Vegas before wind of it reached the IRS—had made the columns a dozen years ago when the *papparazzi* caught them attending the première of *Broken Blossoms*, a remake of a silent soaper that was hyped as Gail Hope's comeback to motion pictures. The prospect of short, ugly, potato-nosed Sam, in tuxedo and fedora and mirrored sunglasses, escorting the cool beauty in spotless white velvet and diamonds had raised all kinds of speculation among the people whose business it is to speculate over such things, then evaporated in direct proportion to the movie's reception among critics and the ticket-buying public. Now the picture appeared occasionally on local TV between "High Flight" and "The Star-Spangled Banner," and Sam Lucy showed up even less frequently, usually in court on charges of conspiracy to commit something-or-other. If Miss Hope and Mr. Lucy were still involved, anybody who tried to put the bee on her was either new in town or tired of breathing.

"So what are you buying?" I asked, "and what's the tariff?"

She reached inside the kneehole of the desk and placed a briefcase on top of it. It was one of those portfolios that women executives carry, tan pigskin with double handles and fine, almost invisible stitching, a couple of hundred dollars' worth of office luggage. I rose a little from my seat and tilted

5

it to see inside. The bundles were banded in paper and laid out with a mortician's attention to propriety.

"Seven hundred and fifty thousand dollars," she said, in the tone she'd used when James Darren dumped her for Debbie Watson in *Hang Ten*. "Give it to Sam and tell him Gail wants out."

I smoked my Winston down to the filter and extinguished it next to hers. "Do you want the briefcase back?"

2

"THE ACTUAL DEBT'S MORE LIKE A MILLION, COUNTING CARS and furs and jewelry and getting set up here," she said. "This is as much as I could raise on this place and the house in West Bloomfield. Anyway, you're supposed to get a break when you pay off early."

" 'Early' meaning before you and Sam walk hand-in-hand through the big gates," I said. She nodded. "What'd he do, forget an anniversary?"

"Sam's been good to me. He used to knock me around a little, but I stabbed him in the back with a serving fork one night and he gave me a Volvo and never hit me again. I didn't figure in the Volvo; I earned that. I did include the fifty grand he spread around to keep the fork story out of the media. He did that strictly for me, bad press being a way of life for him."

She lit another cigarette and pointed it at the ceiling. This time I didn't join her. "I think it started last year when I made Sam late for dinner with a business associate. We were going to the show at the Fisher afterwards so he was bringing me along. I was still drinking then, it was before AA, and I had a hangover the size of Southfield. Anyway we were twenty minutes late. Time enough for two guys in ski masks to go in through the kitchen and plunk the business associate

7

and his companion full of holes while they were waiting. Maybe you read about it.''

"I didn't know Lucy was involved."

"He wasn't, thanks to my head and stomach. But he could just as well have been, and now the only thing that scares the living hell out of me is a dinner date with Sam. The associate's companion was twenty-seven years old, a former Miss Ohio.''

"Why don't you give him the money yourself?''

"Because if I see his face I may not go through with it. I know, he kills people and he steals from the government and when he was younger he did things with a blowtorch I wouldn't wish on Will Hays, but in some ways he's like a puppy, you can't look him in the eye and tell him you're giving him away because the landlady won't let you keep pets. I admit I'm a coward, Mr. Walker. They tell me you've got guts for rent and that's why I called you.''

"It's not his reaction you're afraid of?''

"No. Sam's mellowed, and even when he was younger it wasn't like him to become violent. He was facing two years on a trumped-up stolen credit card rap when he hit me. That would make anyone crazy.''

I stroked the briefcase. It was as close as I was ever likely to come to three quarters of a million dollars. "You've been with him a long time. Unless you're deaf and blind or an idiot you had to have seen and heard things. He might not want to let you go for reasons other than love.''

"I had to consider that, from the men around him if not from him. That's why the money. I'm hoping it will convince him I'm not looking to sell him out. It's unlikely even the federal task force on organized crime would shake loose this much for one witness against one hoodlum. Sam's not Meyer Lansky, or even Myron Floren.''

"There's a cheaper way. You could turn witness against him.''

"Sure, and live the rest of my life as Mamie Underbrush in a prefab house owned by the feds in Salt Lake City or someplace, wetting my panties every time someone rings the doorbell. No, thanks. Besides, I like Sam. I met him at a dinner when I couldn't get arrested in Hollywood. He made me happy, he and his rough friends who looked like truck drivers dressed up for somebody's wedding, and he put up the money for *Broken Blossoms* even if it did stink up the place. He's been good to me and he never treated me like his whore. We whores appreciate that. I just don't want to end up full of holes with my face in the linguini."

"You always did know how to make an impression."

She laughed for real, and this time I heard the waves off Malibu. "Like the time I took a champagne bath at David O. Selznick's sixtieth birthday party. That's when the studio was waxing my hooves to make me the next Jayne Mansfield. Poor Jayne. Six months after she was decapitated in that crash I took a leave of absence and never went back until *Broken Blossoms*. God hates sex symbols."

"This one did okay."

She looked around. "It's a roof. Everyone wants the sixties back, or what they think the sixties were. The club was Sam's idea. I added the bubble-gum touches and the hokey ads with muscleheads in white suits. Fags, the bunch of them. I made sure of that, to keep Sam from getting jealous."

"Does he know you're unhappy?"

"I don't know. You don't slip up on him from behind. He comes on like a lug and dresses like one, but after thirty years in the mill he's got his health and a lot of uptown boys in silk suits and manicures haven't. It isn't all luck." The column of ash on her Bel-Air was two inches long. She tipped it into a tray. "Do you accept the job?"

The briefcase stood on the desk between us. I had to sight along it to see her face. "I charge two-fifty a day, three days up front to cover expenses. Have you got that much left in the jar?"

She produced an industrial-size checkbook from the top drawer, wrote one out, and tore it off. I glanced at it—she dotted the *i* in Gail with a circle, otherwise it might have been a man's signature, no flourishes—and put it in my wallet. "It may take a few days. Meanwhile I'd be more com-

9

fortable if you'd hang on to the cash. The last time I had this much to work with was before they canned me from the board at Chrysler. It's too painful to talk about.''

"I'd rather you took it with you. I know me. The less chance I have to change my mind the better. I read a script on Friday once, thought about it over the weekend, and turned it down on Monday—who'd watch a gangster picture in 1967? They gave the part to Faye Dunaway.''

I scribbled a receipt for the $750,000 and another for the $750 check—three zeroes will change lives and topple governments—gave them to her, and stood up to heft the brief-case. Money never weighs as much as it does. She stood up too, a tiny woman, not much bigger than her posters, who had a way of lifting her chin slightly that made her look like a small girl playing at being grown up. Well, we all were.

I said, "You're not letting me walk out of here with three quarters of a million dollars because of anything L. C. Candy said. Who checked me out?''

"Does it matter?''

"Not for the reasons you might think. I've peeked between too many curtains myself to worry about who's watching my windows. But if he's good enough to find out I can be trusted with a stash this size, he should be good enough to make the delivery himself.''

"It's a fair question.'' She rested five neatly pruned nails on top of the desk. They weren't painted and she didn't go in for those daggers you see around. When you're small I guess it pays to grow everything to scale. "I have ethics too. I don't give out names. He's not in your line, but he knows people and he's not on friendly enough terms with Sam to go running to him with this. Beyond that I wouldn't trust him to hold my cheapest fur coat.''

"He's good,'' I said. "I usually know when someone's sniffing after me. Maybe I'm getting too comfortable.''

"Not on two-fifty a day.'' She tore the top sheet off a pad on the desk with Snoopy in one corner and gave it to me. "That's Sam's home address. Don't give it out. Not that every loyal *Rendezvous* reader didn't memorize it years ago when

10

they ran a two-page spread on the stately homes of the Mafiosi.''

I took a second to burn it in and gave it back. "I hope I won't need it. The last article I read about him had him still working in Southfield. I'll probably make the drop there. They get awful jumpy when strangers come to their homes."

"He's still there. Sam doesn't like change. He never got over Repeal."

"Who did?" I harvested my hat and coat from the tree. "See you in the movies."

She had come around the desk and now she squeezed my hand again with her small strong one. "Call me when it's done."

I went out the suckers' entrance, under the switched-off neon sign. The nightspot had a stale nicotine smell by day, and a bleary, fish-out-of-water look, like a working stiff at home sick in his robe and pajamas watching the soaps. Gray November glowered at me in front of the flamingo, kicked snow in my face. Short of the Canada clippers of January it was about as far as you could get from the beach. So was Gail Hope.

But there was something else out of line besides the season and the time of day, something you couldn't touch but that you knew was there somehow, like a dubbed foreign soundtrack where the actors' words didn't quite match the action. It had my built-in smoke alarm hooting. It hooted all the way to the National Bank of Detroit's downtown branch, where I stuffed two safety deposit boxes with bills and had to come back out of the vault and ask sheepishly for a third before I could empty the briefcase. The female clerk, blonde and pretty in a machine-punched sort of way in a floppy bow tie and football pads, glanced from the expensive case to the cheap suit and said nothing. I lost a little respect for her then.

3

At the tellers' cages in front I conducted a less spectacular but more personally satisfying transaction, depositing four hundred of the $750 Gail Hope had given me in my savings account and turning the rest into long folding. The bills looked more real than the ones I had placed in the boxes. It's like that when you're reasonably honest.

My car, a big gray Mercury with a history and two serial numbers under the hood, the original concealed beneath a steel plate with the new one stamped on it, smelled of old fries and the ghosts of cattle gone to market, reminding me that it was coming on noon and I hadn't eaten since lunch yesterday. I had spent the afternoon turning the foxed pages of pasture-size plat books in the basement of the City-County Building, and the evening following my finger down rows of death notices in the microfilm reading room at the Detroit Public Library, reconstructing the life of a realtor who had died owing people money, which was as interesting as the life got. It had taken two highballs afterward to poke a hole big enough to breathe through in the cake of dust in my throat. The morning call from the Club Canaveral had interrupted a pleasant dream in which I was an archaeologist sifting through the remains of an Egyptian tomb to find out where Pharaoh had skipped with the treasury. It wasn't Indiana Jones but it kept the electricity on.

Being in tall cotton, I tried out a new place on Gratiot for lunch, one of those leafy-lit establishments with brass rails and oak panels and an upholstered bar in the center with flutes and snifters suspended upside-down over it like bats. After five minutes a blue-black brunette in a white blouse and slit black skirt seated me between the rest rooms and the kitchen, where I ordered a New York strip and a cabernet and watched the busy waitresses galloping between tables, ducking trays and one another. I chewed my steak and sipped my wine and admired the choreography.

While I was waiting for the bill I placed a call from the telephone opposite the reservation desk.

"You've reached the Stackpole residence. Leave your message after the beep."

Barry's irrepressible puckishness just would spill over into his recording. I had just started dictating when he came on the line for real.

"Amos?"

"The machine's new," I said. "I suppose you've got a word processor now and everything."

"Don't remind me they exist. Every jerk in the world who has one thinks he can write. Are those bar sounds I hear?"

"There's one in the room. Being on the wagon hasn't hurt your ears."

"Anytime I can't hear ice hit glass I'll move to Tibet. What's your pleasure?"

A long time ago I might have been calling just to talk; but we both knew how long ago that was. "What've you got on Sam Lucy?"

"Not much. I write about organized crime, the sharks and the victims. Lucy's a fat fish in the middle of the school. He's not going any higher and he knows it. He doesn't rate much space in my files."

"Whose files would he?"

There was a cagy little pause on his end. "What's the beef and do I get a cut?"

"You couldn't do much with it. I'm supposed to give him something."

13

"If you're thinking of changing professions, forget it. You think too much before you pull the trigger."

"Nothing that lethal. I'm paying off a debt for a client."

"So pay it. What's to know?"

"He's not expecting it."

"Heavy," he said. "That's like climbing into the cage with a tiger to give him raw meat."

"That's why I need to talk to someone who's counted his stripes. If it turns into anything I'll see you get it. I'm hoping it won't."

"Mitchell Trout."

"What's a Mitchell Trout?"

"It's not a what, it's a who. He's retired now. He used to be Detroit bureau chief for *Rendezvous* magazine. Remember *Rendezvous*?"

"I've been hearing about it a lot lately." Gail Hope had mentioned it three times.

"The old issues look pretty tame now, but in its heyday it made the *National Enquirer* look like *U.S. News and World Report*. The Postal Service shut it down finally for sending pornography through the mails. These days they use racier stuff to sell Pepsi on TV, but pornography never really was the issue. They printed a lot of bad stuff about a lot of famous people. Some of it was true."

"What about Trout?"

"My mentor, after a fashion. It was his stuff about the Detroit underworld that got me interested in the subject. Sam Lucy was his pet story, back when it looked like the Brotherhood might elect him to the national board of directors. Trout infiltrated his eighteenth wedding anniversary party. He was there with a camera when the organized crime task force smuggled Lucy in handcuffs through the back door of the First Precinct on that trumped-up stolen credit card rap. Trout scooped everybody on Lucy's romance with Gail Hope. Remember Gail Hope?"

"In what bar do I find this wonder?"

"No bar." He gave me an address on Sherman.

I took it down in my notebook. "What's his price?"

"If I know Mitch he'll be happy enough to talk about Sam Lucy for free. Tell him I gave you his name."

"Thanks, Barry. How are things at the *News*?"

"Same as ever when I quit last week. That joint operating agreement with the *Free Press* is the death of journalism in this town. I'm back to freelancing, which is a classy way of saying I'm out of work. Anytime you need a one-legged legman, you know where to find me."

"I'd call you ahead of anybody I know with two."

"That's sweet, but you still owe me a piece of whatever it is if it's whatever." The connection broke.

My bill was waiting for me at the table. I paid it and left a twenty percent tip. The service wasn't that hot, but they deserved something for the mileage.

Sherman is inner city, bleached cracked asphalt and shattered sidewalks and weedy lots where pheasants nest, raising streetwise little chicks whose natural enemies are rats and plastic six-pack carriers. The houses need paint and some of them have bullet holes from afternoon drive-by shootings aimed at teenage heroin lords that almost invariably get little girls by mistake. The address Barry had given me belonged to a narrow house built of cement block with tobacco-colored tiles on the outside. The porch roof sagged over a wicker rocker that no one had sat in since LBJ.

I had never seen a copy of *Rendezvous*, but I knew the breed: Photographic covers with chesty starlets hunched forward in gowns cut to their ankles, banners over the logos and down the left side that read JACKIE O. NUDE AT PARTY ON MILLIONAIRE'S YACHT and I'M CARRYING A MARTIAN'S CHILD, dusty brown pulp pages inside with mail-order advertisements offering security work and ninety-day bust-expansion programs and columns with Hollywood datelines based on information supplied by maids and chauffeurs and temporary secretaries. Their time had been brief but purple, a bridge constructed of peepholes between the fan magazines of the forties and fifties and the supermarket trash papers of today. They went with sweaty former newspapermen in windowless rear offices with their sleeves rolled up and their neckties tucked into the front of their pants.

The man who answered my knock didn't look as if he belonged to that litter. My height, built along clean tapering lines in a steel-gray cardigan, pleated slacks, and loafers with a soft sheen like clean oil, he had black hair going gray in front in natural waves and a lean brown face set off by a thin moustache and steel-rimmed glasses. He read my card aloud with a Ronald Colman accent pushed through Kipling and let me into an interior that was as far removed from the face of the house and the neighborhood as Mitchell Trout in person was from the braying moist-palmed world of tabloid journalism.

The furniture was white maple and green plush on a brown-and-ocher carpet that looked Middle Eastern. There were good oil paintings in baroque frames on the walls and a small brick fireplace with logs burning flatly on the grate—half the people who own them don't know how to build a decent fire—and not a television set in sight. Rows of palm-worn books lounged behind glass in a cabinet with a clock ticking on top braced by crouched bronze lions. The clock struck the quarter-hour as Trout was hanging up my coat and hat in a closet off the door, the gears scratching and straining like an old convict trying to cough up a wad of jute.

"Your clock needs a good cleaning," I said.

"It wouldn't keep time any better if I cleaned it. Odd, isn't it, how we continue to wind and maintain them long after we've ceased to trust them? Perhaps it's for the same reason we still read newspapers."

"That sounds like something you'd say to a media convention."

"Media." The moustache crawled. "I reject the term. There is the press and there is entertainment. It's only when we allow them to bleed into each other that we get into difficulty. In any case I'm not invited to speak at conventions. I sold out, don't you know. The *Times*—London, not Ochs's upstart Knickerbocker sheet—Reuters, the BBC—*Rendezvous*? In the eyes of certain of my peers I'd

16

have done better to keep two underage Ethiopian girls locked up naked in a flat in Soho. Sit down, please. I don't have many visitors. Would you object to a martini at this ungodly hour?''

"Shaken, not stirred?''

"Stirred, of course. That blighter Fleming. I knew him when he was with MI-5. Oh, well, the man found his calling in the end, even if he didn't know his drinks.'' He was in the kitchen now, on the other side of an arch by the stairs. Ice crunched from a machine into a steel mixer, liquid splashed, a swizzle went to work with a frenzy. "How is Barry?''

"Freelancing.''

"Sorry to hear it. I offered him a job as a stringer when he came back from Vietnam. That was before he lost the leg. Then *Rendezvous* was shut down before he could answer. I like to think he would have said no. Blast, I'm out of olives. Are you one of those purists who won't have an onion?''

I said an onion would be okay. A minute later he brought out two funnel-shaped glasses containing clear liquid and a pearl onion the size of a cufflink in each. We touched glasses, sipped, and sat down on a pair of green plush love seats set at right angles. He knew how to mix them, which made up for the embarrassment of a fire. Mine tasted like a cold cloud.

"Sam Lucy,'' I said.

"Dear old Sam. What about him?''

"That's my question.''

He frowned over his glass. He had sturdy features: a frank nose with a high curve, a thick lower lip built for frowning, a brow that furrowed in four deep lines without a break. His eyes were true hazel, a color not as common as a lot of driver's licenses would have us believe. "Born Samuel Luschke in Hamtramck, 1922. Sigismund, his father, came over from Cracow in 1918 and drove a beer truck for Yonnie Licavoli. Sigismund died of throat cancer in 1930. After Repeal young Sam ran policy slips for Yonnie, and in 1940 at the age of eighteen he was given the pinball concession in Redford Township. After Pearl Harbor he tried to enlist in the army but was rejected because of a gambling conviction. A year later he was drafted. He was wounded at Monte Cassino, for which he received a Purple Heart. In 1951 he recited the Fifth Amendment at the Kefauver Committee hearings, where he was identified as the juice man for the Detroit mob, the man to see when the machine needed oiling. For a while after Joe Zerilli died, it looked as if Sam might fill the vacancy on the national board of directors, but they went with someone else. He retired a few years later, ostensibly. The term doesn't mean anything more in the underworld than it does in show business. He keeps his hand in, or did until last year. Those are the bare bones.''

"Last year?"

He sat back, swirling his drink. People who do that make my teeth ache. "Feed an old journalist's curiosity."

"It can't get out," I said. "Not until the hide's on the wall."

His features weren't engineered for smiling, but he hung one in front of the frown. "Mr. Walker, if the President fell dead of tertiary syphilis on my threshold and I telephoned it in, they wouldn't print it. The so-called legitimate press threw me out into the storm the day I signed with the enemy."

"I don't think you'd tell them anyway. Gail Hope wants out. You know who Gail Hope is."

"I broke the story on their affair. What do you mean 'wants out'?"

"Out. *O* as in over the wall. *U* as in unfettered. *T* as in truffle, which rhymes with duffel, which is what a grunt carries when he musters out. That brings us back to *out*. She doesn't want any more Lucy. I'm to deliver that message to him along with some cash to clear the books."

"I don't see why she'd bother," he said after a moment.

"She has her reasons. They all have reasons." It sounded a little shrill; the early drink on top of having $750,000 in

18

safety deposit boxes under my name was getting to me. I shut up.

Mitchell Trout wasn't paying any attention to that. "I mean I don't see why she feels she has to do anything. Sam Lucy had a stroke last year, an aneurism. He's been on life support for fourteen months. It's not public knowledge, but he's what you Yanks call a carrot. A vegetable."

4

THE FIRE HAD THINNED TO A COUPLE OF THREADS OF FLAME at one end of the log. I got up, found a poker, and bullied it a little, tilting the log and stabbing at the embers until they got good and mad and took it out on the wood. I put away the poker and returned to my seat. "Who's your source?"

Trout stalled a moment, then moved a shoulder. "Well, you told me the name of your client. It's Lucy's wife, Henrietta. Hank and I go back a number of years. We became friends when the Guerrera brothers were stalking Sam during the cocaine wars and he went underground for a while. I kept pestering her for a line on her husband's whereabouts and she kept having me thrown out until we discovered we have something in common."

"Sam?"

"You're perceptive. Yes, I have a certain affection for Sam. His affair with Gail Hope made me Detroit bureau chief and furnished this place. And Henrietta loves him despite everything. I rather think she appreciated the fact I never set myself up as better than Sam. I wasn't, of course. The techniques he used to gain power and the ones I employed to get a story weren't all that different."

"Did you kill people?"

"As a matter of fact, I did. Would you care for a refill?"

My glass was empty. I stared at it until it meant something. I put a hand over it then and shook my head.

He hung the prefabricated smile on his face. "Not personally, of course. But a number of things I wrote got people killed. Our professions are similar that way, yours and mine. We're catalysts, after all. A lot of questions would not be asked but for us, and the bare fact that we ask them is sometimes lethal. If someone dies so I can write the story or you can satisfy a client, are we any better than the thug who bends an iron pipe over an old lady's head for her Social Security check?"

"Is that why you quit?"

"It quit me. Oh, I suppose I could have found a job after *Rendezvous*; there will always be publications like it and I could have used the income. The investments I had made hadn't begun to pay off yet. I was tired. I was a forty-year-old man who'd spent half his life crouching in damp bushes with a camera or distracting grieving parents at their front door while a partner crept in the back and swiped a picture of the deceased off the mantelpiece. That's colorful when you're young, but after forty it becomes seedy and sad. How old are you, Mr. Walker?"

"Thirty-eight."

"Then you know what I'm talking about. Or you will soon." He drained his glass. "We're confidants, Hank Lucy and I. Widows gossiping over the backyard fence."

"Where is Sam?"

He gave me a room number at St. John's. "I haven't tried to see him. Who wants to look at himself in twenty years?"

"So all you've got is his wife's word."

The air changed in the room then. It was as if a connection had been broken.

"Yes. That's all I've got." Trout was frowning again. He stood. "Tell Barry I said hello."

It was the heave-ho. I got up and shook his hand and thanked him for the information. He opened the door for me and said good-bye, mixing courtesy and coldness with the same precision he applied to his martinis. Someday I'll leave

21

a place without having overshot my welcome; by which time I'll be retired and living alone like Mitchell Trout, although not nearly as well. The thought was small consolation for the conviction that I'd blown a chance at a relationship worth starting.

I didn't dwell very long on it. I had something to check out at St. John's Hospital, namely who was lying to me this time and why.

Hospitals are the best places to approach the insulated in our society. They lock up the drugs all right, but you can get drugs anywhere; while their biggest cash asset, the patients, are exposed to the bright loud thorny world in wards and semi-private rooms without door latches, as cozy as the johnny robes they're forced to wear with the backs flapping open. You can look like Charles Manson on a tear and stroll through the intensive care units gaily kicking out plugs and never get stopped. Unless you're smoking.

I ditched my Winston butt in a potted plant in the lobby that looked to be doing better than most of the people seated there and used the elevator. It stopped on the next floor to admit a tragic-faced woman in her forties wearing a tailored suit and clutching a bright orange teddy bear under one arm with the tag still attached and a young bald orderly with an empty gurney. The orderly was humming the theme from *The Magnificent Seven*.

The doors let us all out into a bright corridor like every other corridor in every other hospital, paved with linoleum as tough as a night nurse and echoing with the padding of rubber soles, the trundling of equipment on wheels, voices rising and falling at the nurses' station down the hall like switch engines dragging the same tired cargo back and forth in a railroad yard, someone coughing dryly and without much hope in a room with the door open—all the canned flat re-heated sounds of life in a sterilized bottle. I passed two nurses walking the other way in white pantsuits and orthopedic sneakers, splitting the air with their stride, and an old woman in a sky-blue robe pulling her way along the wall rail with both hands.

22

Security got a shot in the arm in front of the room I wanted. As I slowed down by the door, a young man with short dark blond hair, wearing a blue suit, rose from a chair by the wall and laid his paperback book open facedown on the seat. He was built to scale and didn't seem very big until I was standing in front of him. He had smooth pale features, a short nose and a long upper lip that made him look younger than he probably was, and dark eyes with long Mediterranean lashes, a contrast to his generally Nordic coloring. Well, the Vikings got around. I glanced at the book he'd been reading. *The March of Folly*, by Barbara Tuchman.

"Must be the new breed," I said. "It used to be *Leather Sheets*, by Anonymous."

He asked me if I was with the hospital. He didn't stutter like an ex-pug and he had no regional accent. I handed him the card I'd gotten out when I left the elevator. He read it without moving his lips, tore it in two, and gave me back both halves. His hands were long and white, with slender fingers. He would be accustomed to doing most of his communicating with them.

I put the pieces in my coat pocket. "Sam Lucy in there?"

He said nothing.

"I don't even have to go inside," I said. "I just want a look at him."

Still nothing. When a man that size says it, it is a lot of nothing.

"Nuts." Carefully I unbuttoned my coat and then my jacket and opened it to show the fat rubber grip of the Police Special in its belt holster. The sight of so much lethal equipment shocked him into silence. He was about to fall asleep on his feet. I'd have bet my car he could get the L-frame automatic that was rubbing a hole in the lining of his jacket out and pumping before I had a hand on the .38.

"Every job has its ethic," I said. "I don't guess body-guarding is different. You're paid to lay down your life. It's a lot of life so I imagine you're getting better than union scale, if you had a union. Large men who can handle themselves come in case lots, so you're also loyal. But you're not

23

working for a man anymore. If Lucy's as bad off as I hear, you've got to have asked yourself if it's worth collecting a couple of holes for someone who can't go to the toilet without General Electric."

A muscle flickered in his jaw.

Half a minute bumped by on square wheels. A gray-haired doctor wearing a white coat over golf greens passed us with a curious glance. It would be the one he reserved for an irregular heartbeat or a rough lie.

"What's the incentive?"

It had been so long since the young man had spoken I had to chew on it for a second. "Secrecy."

"Keep on."

"I just found out today Lucy's been in there fourteen months. That means your employers are spending a lot of money to keep the news from spilling out. Hospitals are full of prowling press. If we get into a hassle here it'll draw attention, someone's going to start asking who's in there that was worth the fuss. Okay, Lucy's retired, but he's got holdings. Whoever put the wraps on needs more time to nail them down before the scrambling starts. He's going to be sore."

"Maybe there won't be any fuss."

"There'll be a fuss."

The square wheels took another turn. He was thinking.

I helped him out. Moving very slowly, I raised my right hand where he could see it and used the thumb and forefinger of my left to lift the revolver from its holster. I worked the barrel up into my hand and offered him the butt. After a beat he curled the slim fingers of his left hand around it.

"Careful," he said, "I could make you crawl to the emergency room from here."

The door to the room was wide, to admit a wheelchair. I pushed down the handle and went in with it, into the thick muted dimness of the room where time lay like a rock in its depression. No one shot me in the back.

5

A STROBE ROCKETED ACROSS THE BACKLIT SCREEN BEHIND the little stage, accompanied by an angry swishing noise like George Reeves used to make when he whipped in through a window on the old *Superman* TV show. In its wake twinkled a green phosphorescence, turning the stage and the walls and the faces above the tables the color of crème de menthe. Then the light show started in earnest, rainbow lasers and *Star Wars* sound effects and a throbbing instrumental rendition of "Sea Cruise." I figured it was safe to light a cigarette.

By the time I discarded the match in the nondescript little period ashtray on my table, the music had stopped with a thump, extinguishing the lights. The stage was black for half a minute or more; long enough anyway for the anticipation to start to break up into whispers and self-conscious giggles. Then a powder-blue spot sprang on over the stage and Gail Hope appeared suddenly from darkness, encased in glossy satin from jacked-up breasts to five-inch stilts and flanked by four tanned miracles of male construction in disco suits and patent-leather boots. The audience gasped. Gail's hair was piled on top of her head and she had on elbow-length gloves that made her look like a blonde Natalie Wood from *Gypsy*. The backlit screen showed a montage of scenes from her leather-and-suntan-oil pictures while she did a few dance turns to "Sea Cruise" that looked trickier than they were

25

because of the hobble-skirt, and the beach boys did some time steps and tried not to knock anything over. The audience hooted and applauded. That ten-dollar cover will do it every time.

I wasn't swept away. As loud as the music got, I kept hearing the climate-controlled silence of a private room at St. John's, interrupted irregularly by the apologetic bleep of the heart monitor. As bright as the lights got, I saw only the forced twilight of a room with the blinds drawn and a pale sunken figure, whiter than the sheets it lay on, with tubes in its potato-shaped nose and wires plugged to its narrow hairless chest and bony left arm and the slow flutter of the chest like a parked butterfly pulsing its wings in the final moments of its seventy-two-hour lifespan. The chest, like the wings, would continue to rise and fall tenuously, quiveringly, rise and fall and rise until—no one could predict when, even within a beat—it would rise and fall the same as it had been doing for hours, days, months; rise and fall and then not rise. The monitor would go to a flat whine and there would be some fevered activity for a while involving oxygen and a crash cart, and then someone would roll back the cobwebby eyelids and a head would shake and the monitor would be switched off and the tubes removed. The body would be wheeled out, the sheets changed, and after fourteen months (or sixteen or eighteen or two years or however long it took) someone else would occupy the bed within hours and it would be as if he had never been there at all.

Sam Lucy. He had ridden in a bulletproof Cadillac and dated a Hollywood movie queen and threatened people with blowtorches and made good on threats. J. Edgar Hoover had called him a cancer, he had had his picture taken with Truman Capote and Castro. What dreams do you dream in a coma? Are they in color, and do they resemble the floor show at the Club Canaveral?

The show ended finally. The lights came up a little and the band, a six-piece mix of aging rockers in clean denims and tie-dyes and young barracudas in Italian sport coats, took over the stage. A few couples got up to dance. A waitress

26

dressed like a carhop came over and took my empty glass and asked if I wanted seconds. I said yes. I couldn't remember what I'd ordered the first time.

It was a whiskey sour, and it came just as Gail Hope joined me in full kit. Sitting down in the dress required some engineering, but she managed it without alerting the vice squad and ordered a tonic water. "Bum a butt?" she asked, when the waitress clattered off. "These things don't come with pockets."

I tossed her the pack. She plucked one out and leaned forward for me to light it, giving me a slant down the front of her dress. She'd aged nicely. She sat back and blew smoke over her left shoulder. "You should've told me you were coming. I'd have gotten you a better table."

"This one's swell."

"So what did you think of the show?"

"Beethoven would've flipped over it. He was deaf already."

"I like quiet places myself. But people don't come here to talk." She looked around, her cigarette pointed at the ceiling. "Half of this crowd wasn't born when the sixties ended. They watch *Easy Rider* and *The Graduate* on their VCRs and get the hippies all mixed up with the antiwar activists and think everyone listened to this music all the time. If I served it up the way it was they'd walk out. Why not? Reality they can get at home."

"That's why I'm paid in advance."

The waitress brought the tonic water and left. Gail sipped at it, put it down. "Needs rye. I didn't expect to see you so soon. What did Sam say when you gave him the money?"

"He doesn't talk much."

"He can talk your ear off when you get to know him, about everything but his work. He can avoid talking about that in two languages."

"Cut."

"I'm sorry?"

"I said, 'Cut.' It's a wrap. Take five. Whatever they say when the cameras stop turning. You're not on a soundstage.

27

Bubble-headed chatter's out of character.'' I took the fold of stiff paper from my breast pocket and laid it on top of the pack of Winstons.

"What is it?" She didn't pick it up.

"It was easier to carry than the briefcase. I'll send that around tomorrow. It isn't my color."

She picked up the money order and unfolded it, looked up at me from the forest of zeroes. Before she could speak I said, "I used my favorite teller for the conversion. The expression I got was almost worth the day lost. I'm hanging on to the retainer, by the way. My time's worth something. About half the cost of that dress."

"You saw Sam?"

"I saw him. He didn't see me."

"I didn't think you'd get to him that quickly."

I had some whiskey. There was more sour in it than spirits, or maybe that was just me. "It's none of my business," I said. "I used to charge just two hundred a day. The extra fifty is the surcharge for being lied to. You paid for the privilege. But it was a lot of cash to let me lug around to buy your freedom from that living waxwork at St. John's."

"It was a test."

I said nothing. The boy in front of Sam Lucy's room had nothing on me.

"I had to know if you could be trusted with this much cash. I used hard currency because it's more tempting." She refolded the money order and tucked it between her breasts.

"Suppose I skipped."

"You wouldn't have gotten far. You were followed."

I watched a couple dancing the Twist near our table. The boy was all elbows and Adam's apple in a shiny black leather jacket and white chinos carefully smeared with grease and the girl had on a poodle skirt and her hair in a ponytail. I wondered if they were following me. It seemed to be the national pastime.

"Where's Lucy figure?" I asked.

"He doesn't. Everything else I said about him is true. He's

28

just not in a position to stop me from leaving him even if I wanted to now."

There was an interior fallacy there, but the music was making my head hurt, so I didn't tinker with it. "I'm bonded up to a million, but I guess you knew that."

"Anyone can post a bond. I had to *know*. Now I do." She put a hand to Fort Knox. "I'm in trouble."

"Um."

"A lot worse trouble than having to get out from under a bad relationship," she continued. "I made a mistake once, a big one. I'm being bled."

"Who'd you kill?"

The music had stopped unexpectedly. I said it loudly and it hung there on the sudden stillness like a sour note on the bass. A couple in early middle age seated at the next table glanced our way, then back. The man said something to his companion. They both laughed.

When the next number started, Gail said, "How'd you know someone was killed?"

"Seven hundred and fifty thousand dollars is a lot of blood. It's the current price in certain circles. You didn't answer the question."

"Not here. Not tonight. I've got another show later. Can you meet me tomorrow?"

"Where?"

"The bookstore in the New Center Building. Take the concourse from the Fisher. I'll be coming in the front door. That way it will look as if we met by accident. Is ten o'clock okay?"

"If that's the hour you like. You bought three days." When she started to rise I touched the back of her wrist. "One lie's all you get. After that we go into overtime."

"I understand. Thank you." She gave me the smile she would reserve for an autograph hound. Then she left.

The band was playing "Dancing in the Street." I didn't hear much of it. My built-in smoke alarm was still hooting.

6

I⊤ was after eleven when I got home from the Club Canaveral. The air inside the house felt as clammy as a wet galosh. The indoor thermometer read fifty-two. I checked the thermostat, which was set at sixty-five, and went down into the little half-cellar, where I spent a cozy hour cleaning the nozzle of the oil furnace that had come over with Cortez and knocking particles out of the filter. I used a twist of burning newspaper to ignite the pilot and hit the reset button. The motor chattered, wheezed, and kicked in with a deep gulp. I screwed the panel back in place and went upstairs to scrape off the soot.

Showered and in a robe, with a glass of Scotch in my hand, I turned on the television set. I was too tired to read and not tired enough to sleep, although it was well past midnight. A talk-show host with an eyetooth grin was interviewing Fats Domino on Channel 2. Channel 4 was playing a Gidget movie and there was a rerun of *Laugh-In* on 7. I couldn't get away from the sixties that night. I turned off the set and sat in the dark with my Scotch until it was gone. Then I went to bed. The house smelled pleasantly of burning oil.

I rolled out at eight-thirty, made pancakes for breakfast, and ate them with honey. I shaved, put on the blue worsted and a light topcoat—the outdoor thermometer read forty-three, six degrees warmer than yesterday's high—and drove downtown to pick up my mail at the office before heading over to the Fisher Building. The mail, waiting for me on the floor under the slot in my little outer office, included a missing-child circular with a five-year-old Xerox photograph on it and a bonanza, the December issues of *Smithsonian* and the *National Geographic*. I put the magazines on the flea-market coffee table and interred a copy of *Time* with Idi Amin on the cover and a *People* of similar vintage in the wastebasket in my private womb. I called my service for messages—they reported none—and flicked the feather duster I keep in the file cabinet at the top of the desk. The motes swarmed around in the shaft of sunlight coming through the open blinds and settled into a new arrangement on the blotter. My morning's business finished, I left.

In the Fisher I passed the usual cluster of jaded business types and jittery radio chitchat guests waiting for the elevators in the tower and took the stairs opposite the guard's station down to the underground concourse. The Art Deco exclamation point of the Fisher Building is connected to the comb-toothed General Motors Building across Grand Boulevard and the New Center Building next door by means of a subterranean walkway, tiled and clean and clanging with the echo of busy footsteps day and night. It's like a little city beneath the asphalt the way Fritz Lang would build it. I walked past a sawhorse by the wall and a man in coveralls on a cigarette break and around the bend toward the New Center Building, where the foot traffic thinned out a little. It was two minutes to ten; I was right on time for my bookstore meeting with Gail Hope. Wood scraped on tile behind me. The break was over, the man in the coveralls was setting his sawhorse in place.

Farther down the concourse, a slender man in a gray suit and belted tan topcoat stopped leaning against the wall and stretched, yawning. It was a real jawbreaker; he'd had a long hard day by ten o'clock. He started briskly in my direction, in a hurry to get somewhere now. His hands slid into the side pockets of his topcoat. I laid my fingers on the grip of the Smith & Wesson under my coat and jacket.

Something hit me hard between the shoulder blades and I stumbled. A foot tried to hook my ankle from behind but I hopped over it, turning to put my back to the wall as I drew the revolver. The edge of a stiff hand struck my wrist at the break and my hand went dead. The gun clattered on tiles.

I was getting stale, all right. If I'd heard the two men coming up behind me at all I'd have classed them as ordinary pedestrians. They were both my size in business suits and light coats and held no weapons. I elbowed the one who had disarmed me in the ribs, but he was backpedaling and the blow skidded off. His companion swung his toe at my crotch. He would be the one who'd tried to trip me. I had my balance now and some feeling in my right hand; I caught his ankle and shoved. He hit the wall deliberately with his shoulder to keep from falling. I jabbed straight out, second knuckles foremost, and connected with his temple hard enough to jar my own teeth loose. He dropped then. I turned to take a bow just as the other one charged in like the Lions' offensive line, all bunched shoulders and the top of a dark head with a bald spot at the crown. The bald spot was all I had time to focus on before my lungs collapsed. I sat down hard.

My hand came down on the gun.

A shell racketed into a chamber then, very loud in my right ear. "Let go of it, Walker."

My lungs inflated slowly, feeding oxygen to my head. The hem of a tan coat drifted into and out of my peripheral vision. The two big men were both standing now, the one who liked to use his feet holding a slim automatic with a fat suppressor screwed to the end of the barrel. I couldn't see the one pointed at my temple, but I calculated the odds that it had come off the same line. I lifted my hand and rested it on my thigh. The revolver was kicked away.

"Steady, men," I said. "I think we may all be working for the same woman."

"I don't think so." The man in the tan coat took a step back—the pistol was a match as I'd thought, right down to the suppressor—and opened a gray leather folder under my nose. The card identified the holder as Special Agent William Sahara. The letters CIA were superimposed on top of the fine print, a little too large for good taste.

7

THERE WAS SOMETHING DIFFERENT ABOUT THE CONCOURSE at that moment besides the proliferation of weapons: We were the only people in it. I wanted to ask about that, but here was the balding fullback who had put me on the floor shoving out a hand to help me up. I took it. He still had all the leverage when with an efficient twist he turned me toward the wall and I had to place my free hand against it to keep my face off the tiles. My feet were kicked apart, not ungently, and he released my other hand so I could put it next to its mate. The frisk began.

"Check all the way down," said the man called Sahara. "He wears an ankle holster sometimes."

"He's clean."

"Sorry, Walker. You have a slippery reputation. You can turn around now."

The guns were all out of sight. Sahara was an inch shorter than I and twenty pounds lighter, more lean than slender, although the cut of his clothes—off the rack but relentlessly altered—softened the angles. He had short brown hair, a straight nose, and a jaw inclining toward the lantern, and he wore aviator's glasses with a light amber tint. The eyes behind the lenses were brown. Not a mahogany brown or a muddy brown or a nut brown, just brown, like the wrapping on an anonymous package. In looks he was as arid as his name, as memorable as a shifting dune; which is how they pick them in Washington.

"My name you know," he said. "This is Earl Moss and Dan Wessell. They're not with the Company but they often help me out when I'm in Detroit."

Moss was the fullback, in his late twenties and running to fat but still muscular, who stood with his box-toed shoes well apart and his arms out from his sides in the classic weight-lifter's stance. Wessell was much thinner, although not thin, with a long neck and a rubber idiot's grin and ears that stuck out under a velour hat with a feather in the band. He had a high crotch and small feet in soft tasseled loafers, well suited for his kick-boxing predilections. He was closer to forty. They looked friendly enough, like killer dogs at rest with their tongues lolling out.

"I thought the CIA had no jurisdiction inside the United States," I said.

"We'll talk about that. We'll talk about a lot of things. But not here. Is anyone in your office right now?"

"How the hell would I know? *I'm* not in my office right now."

"I meant are you expecting anybody."

"Am I?"

Even his patience was forgettable. "Moss, get Walker's gun."

The fullback retrieved it from the wall where it had come to rest, kicked out the cylinder, and tipped the cartridges into his palm. He flipped the cylinder back in place and handed it to me butt first. After all that showy familiarity I wanted to twirl it into its holster like Sagebrush Schultz, but I just stuck it there. I didn't want to spook them into running or drop it on my foot.

Sahara said, "I'll make sure I've lost my tail and then I'll see you back at your office. Moss and Wessell will keep you company." He paused. "Don't worry, you're not standing anyone up. Miss Hope isn't there."

"I guessed that the second I laid eyes on you."

He wasn't one to have to have the last word. He left us,

35

walking in the direction of the New Center Building the way he'd come. I started back toward the Fisher. My escort followed.

When we got around the bed the maintenance man in coveralls spotted us and moved the sawhorse back to the wall. A buzzing clump of men and women in business dress hesitated, then came forward. A sign on the sawhorse read CONCOURSE CLOSED FOR REPAIRS. The dot over the *i* was a round yellow face with button eyes and a smile that reminded me of Wessell's.

"I was wondering how you rigged it," I said.

Moss grunted. "There's another one on the New Center side. The guy there will move it when Sahara shows up." He had a thin voice for his bulk and a delta drawl. A lot of athletes do.

"The happy face was a cute touch."

"Sahara thinks of everything."

"Who the hell *is* Sahara?"

He put a hand under my left elbow and we climbed the stairs to ground level. We were through talking now.

The guard at the station, black with an Errol Flynn moustache and a copy of the current *USA Today* spread before him on the counter, looked up when I paused in front of him. He had on a brown uniform with green patches and a Sam Browne belt with the flap buttoned over the rosewood handle of a chromed Ruger Redhawk. The gun was probably a lot easier to get to that way than if he'd left it on the bus, but it still wasn't encouraging.

"Excuse me," I said. "These two men are kidnapping me."

"Yeah? What's the deal?" His eyes twitched left and right. He was wearing a half grin.

Moss slid his hand up to my bicep and squeezed. I felt a familiar probing against my right kidney. A man ought to know his own gun when it's pointing at him. Under the hum of pedestrian traffic in the marble arcade his murmur died inside of two feet. "I'll blow your spleen through your belt buckle."

"Have a nice day," I told the guard, turning away.

"Fuck you."

We followed the arcade toward the side parking lot. I said, "I'm parked on the street." There were people on the street.

"You're in the lot," said Moss. "We parked one aisle over."

"You guys are good."

"Maybe you're just bad."

"Nah."

My last best chance was the revolving door, but we didn't take it. Moss maneuvered me to one of the others and we went out into the crisp air. I was a little relieved. I've been taken more places at gunpoint than a B actor, and at least it's movement of a kind. Free, I was just another reasonably priced detective adrift between leads. The survivor in me had to keep looking for angles, but the part of me that asks the questions didn't want them. Guns almost always point to answers.

Still another part of me wondered if this was the time they would point to the one answer I could just as soon wait to learn.

I got in behind the wheel of my heap. Wessell let himself in the passenger's side and Moss took the back seat. I caught his eyes in the rearview mirror—lively green eyes with long lashes like a woman's, not at all like Sahara's bland browns—and tilted my head toward Wessell. "Does he talk?"

"Only with his feet. Start the car."

We took Grand to Woodward, drove downtown and then west on Grand River toward my building. At the stoplight on Warren a Metro blue-and-white slid up beside us and the officer on the passenger's side, early thirties with a buzz cut and the ubiquitous shades, turned a bored face my way. Leaning forward and folding his arms on the back of my seat, Moss burrowed the muzzle of my revolver into the right side of my neck. The light changed, we crossed the intersection, and the prowl car turned at the end of the block and left us. Moss sat back.

The hallway leading to my office was empty. There was

37

no light behind the glass in the astrologer's next door, but then I hadn't seen her since the day she moved in, a big woman of sixty or so in man's tweeds with a face like old wallpaper. Office life is like that: The neighbors come and go, you glimpse their lives in flashes as through a window from a moving train, and then it's on to the next.

The door to my waiting room was unlocked, the way I always leave it during the day, and we went on through the press of no clients at all to the private door on the other side, where I fished out my keys. Moss made an impatient sound and reached past me to twist the knob. The door opened.

"You made good time," said Sahara.

He was sitting behind my desk, in just the gray suit and tinted glasses now, having hung his coat on the peg by the door. He had drawn the blinds, casting the office in gray light that enveloped him and almost consumed him. I had to strain to make him out, although it wasn't that dark; it was just the way he was, like a plain rug on a plank floor. If he wasn't born that way he had worked at it a long time. He was in either early or late middle age, and you could meet him three times in one day and not place him from one time to the next, unless he had Moss and Wessell with him.

Moss said, "He didn't give us much trouble."

"That's because he wasn't working at it. Sit down, Walker."

There was no getting comfortable in the customer's chair, which suited me fine. I'd already tagged the brown-and-gray man as one of those sleepy-looking lizards you encounter in the desert that dart from their flat rocks to the meaty part of your leg in the blink of an eye.

He drew a thick envelope from his inside breast pocket and skimmed it at Moss, who caught it one-handed. "Divide that as you like. If I need you again I'll call."

The pair left. I'd miss Wessell.

Sahara swiveled east and west, admiring the battered file cabinet and the olive-painted safe and Miss November on the wall calendar and the print of Custer's Last Stand in its frame next to the door. "I like this office," he said. "It's functional and no nonsense."

"I sent the gumball machine out for repairs just this morning."

"Sorry about breaking in and commandeering your chair. I like to face doors."

"Sorry about the busted spring."

He touched the bridge of his glasses. It was his only mannerism. "Don't think too badly of Miss Hope. She's into the IRS for several fortunes and has no choice but to cooperate. She helped turn Sam Lucy three years ago."

"Turn how?"

"Lucy held controlling interest in a couple of gambling ships off the coast of Chile and had government connections there. A certain high-placed official with Communist sympathies was creating serious obstacles for Company operations in the Andes. He was a devout Catholic. When he didn't show up for church one Sunday his driver went looking for him and found him in his dressing room with two bullets in his chest and a third in his head. That was the driver's story. Later, after he disappeared, the driver was identified as one Jorge Luis Molina, a former blackjack dealer on one of Lucy's ships."

"What did Lucy get?"

"Noninterference in his interstate video game racket, and the chance not to go to prison for using a stolen credit card. That was a little thing the Company cooked up with the federal organized crime task force."

"Tidy." I lit a cigarette.

"Not really. It could just as easily have gone sour and caused an incident. You increase the risk tenfold when you gamble on civilian help. The CIA should have used us."

"Hang on. I thought *you* were the CIA."

He smiled a gray-brown smile. "The credentials are real enough. You could say we work under the Company, but that doesn't mean a Washington file clerk can order around one of our senior agents. Names have a way of showing up in memos, and memos have a way of getting into the hands of

39

the press, so our little group has no name, officially. We're just the clean-up crew the boys in power neckties call in when they don't want to get dirt under their nails. Or anything else. We call what we do counterassassination." He paused. "Does that amuse you?"

I must have been grinning. I felt the tightness in the corners of my mouth. "It just sounds like a lot of unnecessary syllables for a hit squad. Where does Gail Hope figure in?"

"She doesn't. She was a bright bit of bait to see how far you could be trusted. Her—and this." He removed a fold of paper from the same pocket that had held the envelope he'd given Earl Moss and put it on the blotter. I didn't pick it up. I recognized the money order I'd handed Gail Hope. "We have a fairly complete file on you, but files often lie, and money never does. You look disappointed."

"I liked it better when I thought Gail had mortgaged herself to the eyes to buy her freedom. Now that I know it's just this week's allotment for screwdrivers for the Pentagon the money's lost its shine."

"Our sources warned us you're a romantic," he said. "You're still angry over being braced in the concourse. It was the only way I could set up this meeting without word getting back to certain parties. As it was I was followed there, but the sawhorse trick bought me the few minutes I needed. I've since shaken the tail, but tails always come back. Moss and Wessell got anxious when you reached for your gun; I apologize for their zeal." He returned the money order to his pocket and drew out another envelope. I decided he wore his gun on the other side for balance. "There are ten thousand dollars in here. Cash, old bills. They're yours if you can do something for me."

"I don't know any South American dictators."

"I envy you. I don't want to know any more of them. I'm sick of the whole racket. I've had my fill of signs and countersigns and code names and greasy little embassy men with their hands out and bilious congressmen demanding details on clandestine operations so they can broadcast them to their constituents and buy votes. I'm tired of doing business with people I should be putting handcuffs on. If I have to make love to one more lice-ridden slut of a female revolutionary for the freedom of man I'll air-express my crabs to the director in Washington."

"So quit."

"It isn't that easy."

I laid my cigarette in the souvenir ashtray from Traverse City and got up and hung my coat next to his. I took a box of .38 cartridges out of the middle drawer of the file cabinet, unholstered the Smith & Wesson, and loaded it, filling all six chambers. He watched me with sleepy interest. I went around behind the desk and excused myself and opened the top drawer and laid the gun inside it and pushed it shut. Then I returned to the customer's chair and picked up my cigarette. I was ready for the whole sad story.

"We're an independent little group," Sahara said. "True, the CIA itself has no authority in this country, but a dark horse outfit like the one I work for, without official status, is free to work wherever it chooses until it gets caught. Left to his devices in one place for a long enough period, a senior agent like me becomes something of a feudal lord, with his own private army of contacts, informants, and mercenaries like the two you met today. The attitude at the top is that sooner or later these individuals will take it into their heads to cause some damage on their own: strong-arming, extortion, treating with the enemy—well, blackmailing the Company itself for the political dynamite it's placed in his care. Then there are the renegades who write best-sellers. A field man who wants to resign is a burning fuse. A burning fuse has to be snuffed out before it reaches the powder."

"What do they call that, counter-counterassassination?"

He adjusted his glasses. "They already suspect me. That's why I'm being followed. I've been based here five years, two years past the standard rotation deadline. I could disappear, but if I used any of the accepted Company methods of going underground, they'd track me down like a pencil in a drawer. To pull off a vanishing act they've never seen before I need a civilian mind, a good one that hasn't been drilled into the

41

procedural warp. That's where you come in. As I said, I've read your file.''

''Who does the ten grand belong to, you or the Company?''

''It's mine. I borrowed the seven hundred fifty thousand from the discretionary account. Seed money. I've bought presidents for less. Do you want the job? I don't mind telling you I've gone to considerable lengths to consult with you. Far more than you know.''

''I wouldn't know what to do with ten thousand dollars, Mr. Sahara. Is that your name, by the way?''

''It's the one I'm using at present. The money isn't meant to tempt you. If this works I'll consider it well earned. I thought perhaps you might be swayed for reasons of sentiment.''

I felt the tightness again in the corners of my mouth. ''Flag and country?''

''Wife and home. For a little while, anyway.'' He touched his glasses a third time. ''We're related in a way, you and I. I'm married to your ex-wife.''

8

I PUT MY CIGARETTE OUT CAREFULLY, SQUASHING IT INTO A lump on top of Grand Traverse Bay and using the lump to tramp out the last glowing spark. "Where is she?"

"In the area. I wouldn't advise a visit. She's under surveillance too."

"She gave you my name?"

"Not in connection with this. She mentions you from time to time, although not as often now as in the beginning. We've been married three years. I knew you were a private investigator, and she was willing to admit you were dedicated. The rest I got from your file."

"Last I heard she was in Aruba helping somebody spend his inheritance."

"She returned here when that blew up. It was before we met, but I know most of the details. I investigated her past. That's when I first came across your name."

"Being a spy sure comes in handy in the romance department."

"We have to be careful about our associations. Actually, I ran the check before I developed a personal attachment. I first saw her four years ago at a fifteen-hundred-dollar-a-plate dinner at the Hyatt Regency in Dearborn. For world hunger, if you can believe it. Her escort later used the money raised there to buy guns to sell to the rebels in El Salvador. He's

43

doing eight to twenty now in the federal corrections facility in Marion, Illinois.''

"Congratulations.''

"It wasn't my bust. I just kept track of his movements while he was here and passed the information on to Washington, including what I'd learned about his lady friend. The job isn't *all* killing. Anyway, something about Catherine interested me apart from the bare facts of her life—maybe I don't have to tell you what it was—and I looked her up six months later. Six months after that, we were married.''

"Sweet of her not to hold it against you for throwing her boyfriend in the slam.''

"He wasn't her boyfriend, just someone she'd met and a chance to dress up for the evening. When she was questioned she claimed ignorance of his activities, and our information confirmed that. Women get caught up in these things. It's one reason most field agents are male. There are definite advantages.''

"Brings a whole new meaning to the phrase 'service of your country.' '' I looked at Custer. "Catherine always had lousy taste in men.''

"I wasn't aware from your file you'd given up on yourself.''

"I meant the men she ran around with. She's an adventuress, or she was when I knew her. Not too many of those left. They went out with silk bodices and schooners.''

"I sensed that in her. Maybe it gave me a head start: James Bond and all that. You haven't once asked how she is.''

"Fine, I suppose. She always took care of herself first. Is she disappearing with you?''

"No. The first rule of going underground is you have to cut yourself off from your past life entirely.'' He raised and resettled his glasses. "You may as well know that things haven't been good between us for a long time. That's not why I'm dropping out, but it's made the decision easier. Naturally she'll be provided for.''

"Naturally.'' I picked up the envelope from the blotter, thumbed through the frayed $100 and $500 bills, took out a thousand, and gave him back the rest. "This buys four days: expenses. If it takes longer than that I'll come back for more. This—and one other thing."

His amber gaze hardened. "You can't see her. She's being watched too closely. I can't use you if the Company finds out we're in contact."

"I don't want to see her. I want my file."

"Your file, why?"

"I'm fascinated by me. Can't get enough of myself. I want every copy of every document, every picture and negative. The memory banks wiped clean. Six weeks from now when somebody feeds my name to a government computer, I want it to kick out a big fat question mark." I caught a glimpse of Custer's uniform. "On second thought, you can leave my service record; that's public property. Everything else goes. Can you do it?"

"The people who compile those things will just get back to work and in two years the record on you will be nearly as complete."

"I'll take the two years. I didn't hang those blinds because I was afraid someone would break in and steal the dead moths out of the light fixture. Can you do it?"

"I don't know. I've falsified reports and destroyed papers, but that was when they were still in my hands, before they went into the mill. Are you sure you wouldn't rather have the ten thousand?"

"It would just put me in a tax bracket. Can you do it?"

"I wish you wouldn't keep saying that."

"Can you do it?"

"Yes, damn it. I'll have to call in some favors."

"The telephone's in front of you."

"Now?"

"Later you'll be vanished. If I work it right *I* won't be able to find you. That's what you want, isn't it?"

He laid a hand on the receiver. "Give me twenty minutes."

I got my coat, went to the delicatessen down the street, and drank a cup of coffee. A pair of young women in rabbit

45

coats seated at the next table were discussing trying out for parts in something by Ibsen at the Attic Theater. One of them stopped emoting long enough to ask me to put out my cigarette. We were in the smoking section, but I obliged. The neighborhood was changing. The next thing you knew they would plant trees along the sidewalks and drive away the working girls on the corner, and what street trade I had would dry up and blow away. I considered consulting the lady astrologer about a change in careers. Maybe Ibsen had something for me.

Sahara was still talking on the telephone when I got back. I sat down in the waiting room and started an article about dinosaurs in the *National Geographic*, but that was too depressing, so I returned it to the coffee table and blew smoke at my framed *Casablanca* poster. Just then Sahara poked his head out of the office. "Well, there's no going back to Washington now."

"Did you do it?"

"I had to promise some things I won't be able to deliver on from hiding. I'll have the file by the end of the week."

"Thanks. Let's talk details." I patted the settee adjacent to my chair. A fine puff of dust coughed up. He chose the chair facing mine, which gave him a view of the door to the hallway. "Who's following you and on whose orders?" I asked.

"I'm not sure who's doing the following. That suggests someone in particular, because if it were anyone else I'd have gotten a look at him by now. I haven't lasted twenty years in this work by being inept. This one's less so. His name's Usher."

"Roderick?"

"Frank. Short for Franklin. He prefers to be called Papa. He's pushing sixty—not unheard of in the field, but rare enough to underline in his jacket. That should tell you something."

"Is he a killer?"

"We're all killers. This one made his bones infiltrating the black market in Vienna for the OSS after World War Two. I pulled his picture from the file." He took it out of his handkerchief pocket and gave it to me.

It was an old-fashioned portrait with a soft focus. I looked at an ordinary face, somewhat plump, with smoky eyes and dark thinning hair in a widow's peak and a neat little moustache. The face could have belonged to a clerk who had been passed over for promotion so many times you could see footprints on his forehead. "How long ago was this taken?"

"Nineteen sixty. He hasn't posed for one since, and if there were ever any candids he's burned all of them. He doesn't have a standard ID because he refuses to sit for the picture."

"What's he look like now?"

"I don't know. We've never met and there was no description in his file. He has cheap taste in clothes, that much I can tell you, and he sometimes carries a stick, but it's just show. Papa's a special case. Our little group was built around him, the way you build a road around a shaggy old oak because it's too much trouble to cut down and blast out the stump. Also he's good. That's why he's as old as he is. Some of the younger agents think he's just a legend, one of those bogey stories rookies get told as part of their initiation. He's real enough, all right. Thirty or forty witnesses would swear to it, if they weren't all dead."

I put the picture in my shirt pocket. "Can he cross running water, and will ordinary bullets work on him or should I have some made out of silver?"

"I just don't want you complaining to me later I didn't tell you how bad it can get," he said. "I'm not even sure he's the one tailing me. I hope I'm wrong. Shadow men come cheap. Papa doesn't get on you unless he smells blood in the water."

"You didn't answer the second part of my question. Who sicced him on you?"

"Some desk pilot in Washington. Take your pick, they punch them out of a big sheet."

I asked a few more questions. When I had enough to fly

47

on, I stood. "Let me set some stuff up. Where can I reach you?"

"Leave a message if I'm not in. There's a machine." Rising, he handed me a stiff white card with a whorled surface bearing the legend JEROME BOSCH, COUNSELOR AT LAW and a city telephone number in shiny black characters.

"Who's Bosch?"

"Nobody. You don't think I put my own name on business cards."

"Hieronymous Bosch. *The Garden of Earthly Delights.* Cute. Would Usher know you're an art connoisseur?" I put the card away with some others in my wallet.

"I'm not. I took an art survey course twenty years ago in college and that's all that stuck. I cover my tracks better than that." He studied me. His scrutiny had all the disturbing power of screws in a strikeplate. "Was it Catherine that decided you to take the job?"

"I think about Catherine as often as you think about Bosch. It so happens I'm not up to my hips in clients just now; it so happens that happens pretty often. I don't like to do crossword puzzles and I've got a winter property tax payment due next month. And you and the Twins from the Tunnel will probably go on bracing me in embarrassing places until I agree to help you, so why not cut my losses?"

"You're a liar," he said in a friendly tone.

I moved a shoulder. "I didn't care for it myself."

"I won't say it's none of my business. I've made a business out of things that are none of my business."

"Maybe I think a man should be able to quit his job when he wants to without getting killed for how well he did it. Or maybe it's because of Gail Hope."

"She has nothing to do with this. She was just handy."

"Maybe she's tired of being handy."

He smiled after a second. It transformed his face not at all. "Better. I suppose I am her last link to the Company. Whoever they send to replace me won't remember the Lucy case. She's one washed-up movie queen who might not mind being forgotten."

48

I waited while he went back into the private office and came out carrying his topcoat. He saw I was waiting. "Say it."

"I can be suckered," I said. "I bat five hundred in that park. That doesn't mean I like it. The next time you turn your dogs loose on me I'll hurt one of them or both of them. You I won't fool around with. You I'll kill."

"It's been tried."

"It only has to work once." I opened the hallway door. "Be packed when I call. We may have to move fast."

He went out, letting me have the last word again. It made me feel cheap, but only for as long as it would take him to reach the second flight of stairs. Then I went out after him.

9

ONE OF THE ADVANTAGES OF FOLLOWING SOMEONE IN YOUR own building is knowing which boards squeak and which steps wobble because the super hasn't held a hammer since Eisenhower. I avoided all of them and reached the foyer just as the front door was closing against the pressure of the pneumatic tube.

He had the tan coat on now and was walking east on Grand River, not hurrying but not wasting time either. His walk was as indistinctive as the rest of him. He was better than invisible, he was wholly unnoticeable. If his clothes had been any neater he'd have stood out; if his appearance had been any more drab he'd have called attention to himself. I wondered if he spent an hour in front of the mirror every morning, searching his person for anything that looked as if it hadn't been milled in a factory before he went out, or if the camouflage came so naturally now he never even thought about it. Wondering that, I almost lost him. He blended into the unremarkable scenery of the neighborhood like a paper clip.

I spotted him again as he stepped off the sidewalk. He looked both ways while I made myself insignificant—although not as much so as he—in a doorway, then crossed the street, unlocked the driver's door of a dust-blue Chrysler parked on the other side and got in. I stayed in the doorway and took down the license number as he levered the car out into traffic. It didn't spell anything.

Back in the office I parked a hip on the desk and called Floyd Latimore at the local branch of the Secretary of State's office. A catatonic civil servant of uncertain gender put me on hold and Floyd's late-adolescent voice came on a minute later. He'd celebrated his fifty-second birthday in July. "Amos, you find an honest line of work yet?"

"I had my eye on a TV pastorship," I said, "but that went sour. I need a name to go with a number on a license plate."

"Call the cops."

"It isn't police business yet."

"Lansing gets awful sore when we give that information out to the private sector."

"I didn't call Lansing, Floyd, I called you. Do I have to go into why?"

"Don't be shrill. Let's have the number."

I read it to him. Floyd had come to me some time back with a note from a first wife he had not quite managed to divorce before he married his second, demanding money to prevent her from charging him with desertion and bigamy. I'd done a little digging and turned up a husband the first wife had misplaced, still waiting for her to return from her hairdresser's since before she'd met Floyd. I sent a photocopy of the marriage certificate to the return address on the blackmail letter and Floyd never heard back from her. It was a break for us both: now that John Alderdyce was an inspector he didn't hardly associate with no rental heat, and I needed a pipeline to the computers that matched names to license plate numbers.

"Twenty minutes," Floyd said, after he'd read it back to me.

"Why so long?"

"Machines go to lunch too. I'll call you."

I thanked him and went down the street for a BLT and advice from my waitress, a former nurse, on the care and feeding of the human heart. The telephone was ringing when I let myself back into the brain box.

51

"Magoo, you need glasses," said Floyd without greeting. "You wrote down the number wrong."

"Who's it belong to, the governor?"

"It belongs to Yehudi. No such plate has ever been issued to any car registered in this state. You sure it was Michigan?"

"Yeah." A cheek got sucked on. "What would it take for someone to get hold of a nonexistent registration number?"

"Outside of stamping the plate himself, I couldn't say. For that he'd need the equipment and reflecting paint, and the paint's just a little easier to lay hands on than the ink they use to print currency in Denver. Oh, but then any cop who happened to run the number would pull him over once he drew a blank. The guy's better off standing in line with the rest of us suckers and paying the two dollars."

"Do the cops use your computer?"

"Not directly. The city and county computers are plugged into the state police and *their* computer's wired to the Secretary of State's office in Lansing."

"What if there's a hold order in the state police computer when certain registrations numbers are fed to it? The cop runs the plate, the dispatcher gets the word and tells him to pass this one by?"

"Who are we talking about, the Swiss ambassador?"

"Just spitballing, Floyd. I probably got the number wrong." I lit a cigarette. "How are things at home?"

"I wouldn't know. I'm living at the Holiday Inn in East Detroit."

"What happened?"

"Arlene found out about Robin."

"I thought your first wife's name was Lois."

"Far as I know it still is. Robin is the woman I'm engaged to."

I blew smoke over the Little Big Horn. "Floyd, there's an order to these things. Unless Arlene has another husband stashed somewhere like Lois did, you're headed down a long dark hole."

"Oh, I'm divorcing Arlene. She just didn't know it until recently." The line clicked twice; he had another call on his end. "Don't screw up next time, okay? I'd hate to lose this job over a wrong number."

We hung up. I finished my cigarette in thoughtful silence, or in silence anyway. Floyd's private life was worse than Omaha Beach, but he didn't make mistakes on the job. And I hadn't gotten a license number wrong since George Burns was in short pants. Bill Sahara, whoever he was, drove around with a plate that was as untraceable as his name and description. That at least was a grain on his side of the scales. The first part of any investigation is spent separating the slugs from the genuine coin, and so far this one rang true enough to proceed to the second part.

Private eye evolution ought to include a leather behind and document-dust filters in the nostrils. Not possessing those improvements, I squirmed and sneezed away an hour in my second home, the third seat from the door of the microfilm room at the library, scrolling through the obituaries from the *News*, *Times*, and *Free Press* from 1948. The choice of years was a little better than a crapshoot. Sahara had mentioned being in college twenty years ago, and the average age of a graduating senior then as now would be twenty-two. In any case I wasn't estimating aircraft measurements for Boeing.

The *Times* had what I was after, in its Tuesday, July 6 edition:

Benjamin Boyer, aged 2 mos., 11 days: Born April 24, 1948, to Julius Glynn Boyer and Marian Bernadette (Shepherd) Boyer of 1523 Woodrow Wilson Court; died Monday morning at home of respiratory failure. Survivors, in addition to his parents . . .

I took a moment to think about Julius and Marian: placing the notice, picking out a little coffin, painting over the clowns on the nursery walls in silence. Maybe there weren't any clowns. Maybe there wasn't a nursery. Maybe Julius and Marian had never wanted a child in the first place and took off for Europe to celebrate. Maybe I ought to lay off the private emotions of others, at least until I finished robbing the grave. I wrote down what I needed and went from there to the City-County Building, where I asked a clerk in Records with a Knights Templar pin on his lapel to look up the 1948 birth certificate on one Benjamin Boyer. He made a nasty face and told me to come back tomorrow. I offered him the Masonic handshake. He took it after a second and asked me to wait. The handshake was all I'd gotten in payment from a Manufacturers Bank vice president for pulling his sixteen-year-old daughter out from under a bass guitarist in Grand Ledge; this was the first time it had bought me anything, but then the daughter had run away again anyway after two weeks and I'd told the vice president to find another sleuth. I read a poster warning me to stay away from Laetrile and when the clerk came back with the certificate I paid him a fee to make two copies on official stock. I got out of there at the price of another handshake.

In my office again I broke a blank application form out of the file cabinet, filled it out, and stuck it and one of the copies in an envelope, which I stamped and addressed to the Social Security Administration in Washington. I filed the other copy and went down and slotted the envelope into the mailbox on the corner. In ten days to two weeks I'd have a Social Security card in Ben Boyer's name, which would get Sahara work anywhere. I didn't think Ben would mind.

I'd earned a drink, but I had a sudden thought. I went back upstairs, took the other copy of the birth certificate out of the files, looked around the office tapping the edge of the folded paper against my teeth, and stood on my chair to poke it into the glass bowl of the ceiling fixture. The rectangular outline showed through the milky glass when I turned on the light, but not obviously; the building cleaning service never dusted above eye level. I locked up and went out.

Later I congratulated myself, but at the time it was just routine paranoia.

10

I WAS BUSY FOR THE NEXT FEW DAYS. FIRST I PAID A visit to a camera shop I knew on Chalmers, where for fifty dollars the owner went into his back room and drew up a temporary driver's license and stamped out a Visa card, both in the name of Benjamin Boyer. With them I opened charge accounts in three department stores with branches across the country, then burned them in my wastebasket; phony IDs are time bombs, and Sahara would have the genuine articles soon enough. Then I drove out to Ann Arbor, asked some questions around the University of Michigan campus, and made certain arrangements with an attendant in the medical school there. That cost two hundred dollars. Finally I paid a call on Albert Schindler in his East Side garage.

I found him relaxing for once, drinking a Coke in his neat little office with the gray steel desk and the boxes of new spark plugs and headlamps and seat covers arranged alphabetically on shelves. He had the head of a poster boy for the SS—clean fair profile and curly blond hair—and the body of a Morlock. I had never seen him in anything but coveralls and suspected he had given up trying to find clothes to fit his apelike arms and torso and stunted legs. His left foot, resting on an outdrawn desk leaf, turned inward forty-five degrees, a congenital defect that didn't slow him down any more than an ingrown toenail. He was almost sixty and looked barely thirty. An old-fashioned Zenith radio with a gaudy dial was playing chamber music on the desk.

"Walker." He kept his seat. "Did that rolling boiler blow up on you finally?"

"You're just sore because I didn't buy it from you." I sat down in a clean plastic scoop chair and swung a leg over my knee. Everything was clean in the garage. You could eat off the floor under the hoists if you didn't mind getting yelled at for not using a placemat. "As a matter of fact, I need a car, but it isn't for me."

"I'm a mechanic, not a dealer. You passed six of them on your way here."

"They want paperwork. All I want is a clear title."

"Oh. That kind of car."

"Something old, but in good shape. It doesn't have to look like much, but I don't want it getting pulled off the road as a rolling disaster area. It should perform without calling attention to itself."

"Plate?"

"Dealer's temp will do. It's just to get someone out of the area."

"Price range?"

I gave him five bills. The Sahara money was getting low. "That's to get you started. I'll settle up when you hand me the keys."

"What's the name on the title?"

"Benjamin Boyer." I spelled it.

"I'll call you."

I left him, a real treasure. He knew more about automobiles than Henry Ford and had a son who was always in trouble.

I used the pay telephone in the garage to check my answering service. The post office had called to say that an express package was waiting for me at the Fort Street branch.

I parked in a slot for postal vehicles only and went in after it. It had no return address. Back in my car I opened the red, white, and blue container and drew out a manila envelope with something inside it the size and shape of a photo album. I peeled up the flap and slid a gray cardboard file folder into my lap. The tab read WALKER, AMOS in neatly printed block capitals.

I didn't open it there. I drove back to the office and locked myself in and poured Scotch into a pony glass from my private desk stock and stretched out on the old backless sofa with the reading lamp on.

Some of it had been typed on cheap drugstore stock. Other information had been printed out on green-and-white computer paper in foggy dot-matrix. There were old newspaper clippings in which someone had highlighted my name with a yellow felt-tipped marker. There were medical reports. There were canceled checks with my endorsement on the backs. There weren't many of those. There was a copy of my first application for an investigator's license, which belonged in the Smithsonian. There were photographs and negatives. These included a couple of headshots from old licenses, a candid in a crowd of cops I recognized from the *Free Press* at the time of the Alonzo Smith shooting, several I had never seen that looked as if they had been taken with a long lens from a distance, a couple I had obviously posed for but didn't remember. Here I am at my wedding. Here I am in my specialist's uniform. Here I am in front and profile at the jail in Iroquois Heights, looking like Jimmie Jones after the lemonade.

I looked at all of them. I read everything. Date of birth, check. Height 6'1", generous by half an inch. Weight 185. Hair and eyes brown. One-centimeter scar on lower lip—fell out of a treehouse, Doc, age nine and a half—old surgery scar on right side of abdomen, to pin together a rib splintered by a bullet. Slight protrusion at bridge of nose, an old break—dropped my guard in the second round, Coach, they hit hard in college. *Military service*: Two years Vietnam and Cambodia, First Air Cavalry, three years stateside, Military Police. *Education*: B.A. Sociology, eleven weeks in the Detroit Police Department's cadet training program, the Tet Offensive. *Associations, Personal*: None. *Associations, Professional*: John Alderdyce, Inspector, Detroit Police Department; Barry Stackpole, journalist; Lee Horst, information broker; Lou Gallardo, repo man. The list seemed short. At that they were the closest thing I had to friends in Detroit, and I didn't know anyone outside Detroit. *Habits*: Cigarettes (Winstons exclusively), Scotch (in a bottle), following one slightly bent snoot into deep sewage. *Turn-ons*: Old movies, dead female vocalists, people in trouble. Kisses on the first date, but doesn't go all the way. Like dogs, tolerates cats if they're sufficiently doglike. Good cook, indifferent dresser. Never met a pickpocket he didn't like or a union rep he did. *Turn-offs:* Barbershop quartets, colorization, reading files with his name on them.

I finished it in an hour and a half, getting up twice to refill my glass. The telephone rang on one of these trips but the caller hung up when I answered, another wrong number. When I turned over the last leaf I put it all back into order, carried the folder into the little water closet, and shook its contents into the toilet. I threw the folder in last. I squirted half a can of lighter fluid over the pile, struck a match, held it a moment until it burned down past the sulfur, and dropped it into the bowl. The fluid went up with a polite little thump. I watched the pages shrivel and crawl, the couple in the wedding picture writhe together and melt into a flaming black hole. When I was sure the stuff wouldn't clog the pipes I dropped the lid and pushed down the pedal. As the water gushed and growled I lifted my glass and drank what was in it. It was one of the better and wetter wakes I'd been to.

I went back to the desk and sat down. I didn't feel born again, or even cleansed. I felt as empty as the tank, or as empty as the gesture, which was emptier. It brings no great lift to see one's life boiled down to a half-inch sheaf of papers in a cardboard folder, filed along with all the other half-inch lives in a drawer like the ones they have at the morgue. A life that is all murmurs and images can always be changed. Write it down, collate and cross-reference it, and it is there forever, the letters like uniform headstones in a bureaucratic Arlington, their sounds and meanings embalmed and entombed in concrete vaults, enshrined, immobile. If the first cave-dweller who had stopped boasting about his day's hunt over the fire to set it down in charcoal on the granite wall of his boudoir had been pinioned and trussed and fed to a tiger by his outraged companions, we would all be better off, our sins and mistakes as erasable as those marks on a child's magic tablet that vanish when the cellophane is lifted. Shakespeare had it wrong: First kill all the clerks.

No matter how well you live your life, the thought that all the smudges and half-measures are part of the permanent record is shameful, like waking up from a private erotic dream to find that others have been watching and listening as you thrashed and muttered. You try to forget and sometimes you succeed, but now and then on the edge of your hearing you'll detect the furtive scribbling, like rats' claws on plaster.

The telephone rang again while I was examining the bottle and wondering whether the rest of the afternoon was worth not sacrificing to the great twin gods J&B. I left the decision to whoever was on the other end.

At first there was no one on the other end, just as before. I started to hang up.

"Amos?"

It was just another woman's voice, heard on an instrument that had brought me plenty of women's voices in every key since the day I'd had my name painted on the office door; the team that had assembled the dossier that had blistered the underside of my toilet lid might have been able to estimate their number. If I hadn't just been reading the file and wasn't still stuck in reverse gear, I

59

might not have recognized it at all. Then again maybe I would have even if I'd been up to my neck in the present.

"Hello, Catherine," I said, screwing the cap back on the bottle.

11

"YOU ALWAYS DID HAVE A MEMORY LIKE AN ELEPHANT," she said after a pause.

"Elephants have the hide for it," I said. "They're born with it. I had to make mine from scratch." I waited.

"So how are you? How's Dale?"

"Compared to Dale I'm swell. He's been dead for years."

"Oh." At least she didn't say she was sorry. She had only one face, however much time she spent on it in the course of a day. "Did you get a new partner, or are you all alone?"

"Sometimes there's hardly enough business for one."

"You're alone?"

"What's on your mind, Catherine?"

She feigned irritation to cover the real thing: same old Catherine. "Aren't you going to ask me how I am?"

"How was Aruba?"

"Too many beaches. I'm lucky I don't have skin like barn siding. I've been back a long time. Years. I'm in Detroit now." This time *she* waited, but I didn't jump in. She gave up. "I wasn't doing anything and I got to wondering about you, what you were up to and if you were still in town doing the same thing. First I looked up Apollo Investigations. It wasn't listed."

"I changed the name after Dale was killed."

"Dale was killed?"

"So you looked me up under my name and here we are talking."

Long pause. She would be looking at her nails the way she did—her perfect nails—as if the next line were written on them. It's funny the things you remember. "I know Bill went to see you," she said.

"Who's Bill?"

"My husband, William Sahara. Don't pretend you never heard of him. You never could lie to me."

"I never tried." I hadn't this time, either. It was hard to think of Sahara as anybody's Bill.

"Are you saying you haven't seen him?"

"If you think he's sneaking around you might consider hiring a private investigator. I can give you some names."

"Did he hire you to follow me?"

My chair squeaked. "Hold on a second."

"What?"

I laid the receiver gently on the blotter and got out my handkerchief to wipe my palms. Both palms were dry. I looked at the bottle again and shook a cigarette out of the pack instead. I lit it and picked up the receiver. "What was the question?"

"You heard me," she said.

"Would he have a reason to have you tailed?"

Another pause, shorter this time. "Amos, can you get away for a drink?"

"A drink I can do right here in the office."

"Please, Amos."

The cigarette tasted like an overheated radiator. I put it in the ashtray and let it smoke itself. "Where do you want to meet?"

"I've been out of circulation a long time. Most of the places we used to go to are probably closed by now. You pick. Someplace we can talk."

"I know the place," I said.

I missed the first half of the floor show. The hostess, a tall blonde dressed lke Marilyn Monroe in a spaghetti-strap dress she had put on with a roller—to distinguish her from the waitresses dressed like carhops—seated me near the busboys' stand, shouted in my ear that I'd be served after the show, and sashayed out of my life. I watched Gail Hope and the Malibu Mafia make a few taps and turns look like a production number out of *Guys 'n' Dolls* and listened to the applause washing over like breakers in the second of pitchblackness that came on the end of the last drumbeat. When the lights came up, Catherine was standing by the table.

"You're getting gray," she said.

I stood up. She had on a suit made out of a used dropcloth that would have run three figures, all bright daubs and spatters on some stiff material like canvas with shoulder pads and a skirt that caught her at mid-calf, over a red silk blouse and a goldstone necklace with beads the size of cueballs. Her pumps were gold, too, and it brought out the highlights in her hair, which was auburn now and almost shoulder-length; but then the tomboy cut I remembered was as dead as Nehru. She seemed to have on no make-up at all, which meant she had put on the right kind for the lighting in the Club Canaveral. Leave it to Catherine to show up dressed and painted correctly for a place she said she had never been to before.

"I've got a painting of me that never gets gray at all," I said. "The artist screwed up my instructions."

"I see you still have your sense of humor."

"You always did hate it." I pulled out her chair.

She remained standing. "Is this the best table you could get?"

"If it were, you still wouldn't like it. We're not here for the show." I got her into the chair finally and took my seat. A carhop wobbled over. I looked at Catherine. "Is it still a gimlet?"

"Only in the summer. Seven-and-Seven, please. The gentleman will have red-eye."

"In a clean glass," I said. "I'm civilized now."

"Excuse me?" The hop looked panicky. She was a little redhead with a bar of freckles like a wicker fence across both cheeks. She wore a navy jacket with gold buttons and epaulets, a red pleated cupcake shirt that ended with her pelvis, red high heels, and a cookie-tin hat set at a dangerous angle.

"Scotch and soda."

She clattered off and returned a few minutes later with the drinks. Catherine lifted hers. "We have an anniversary coming up."

"I don't celebrate until January," I said. "That's when I got the letter from your lawyer."

"Amos, let's not fight."

I looked at her like a detective. She had lost weight, quite a lot of weight. She had never been fat or even plump, but when the fashion went from Botticelli's Venus to Gertie the Amazon she would have gone right along with it: Nautilus machines, designer leotards, the works. Her face had lost its girlish roundness, which was one of the things that had attracted a young would-be sociologist with his draft notice in his wallet. Her eyes were gray and tilted away sadly from a Grecian nose, bold and straight. Her forehead was quite high, giving her face the illusion of length, and she had a tiny pale star-shaped scar on her right cheekbone, from a fall off a high school balance bar onto an exposed bolt. The fall had changed her plans to become an Olympic gymnast. If it hadn't, something else would have.

"I'm surprised you didn't get rid of the scar," I said.

She touched it with a coral nail. "You used to like it."

"I still do. That's why I'm surprised you didn't get rid of it."

"I've learned to live with my imperfections. Have you?"

"Are we talking about yours or mine?"

"I was just getting used to the ones you had when you went over there," she said. "You came back with an entirely new set."

"The old ones didn't work anymore. That happens after you've shot away a thirteen-year-old Asian's face with an M-fifteen."

She flinched. "That's one of the things I was talking about," she said bitterly. "Does it make you feel better to horrify me?"

64

"Talking about it was the only cure I had. I wound up talking to the refrigerator while you went to the movies."

"You talked to Dale Leopold. *He* talked you into signing up for another hitch as an MP. You threw away your education to become a cop. I'll never forgive him for that."

"It was either Dale or my service piece."

"Don't overdramatize yourself. You were going to join a welfare agency and help people. Instead you run around after husbands and wives and take pictures through keyholes. Oh, hell, would someone please ring the bell before we kill each other?" She glanced around at a busboy rattling crockery on the stand.

"We're both out of training," I said. "We used to draw a bucket of blood before anyone yelled uncle."

She lifted her drink. "To—what, reunions? Or rematches?"

"Imperfections." I took the top off my Scotch.

She sipped and set her glass down. "I guess you're not married."

"Guessing suits you."

"Any particular reason, apart from the mess we made?"

"The honeymoon would wipe out my bail fund."

She wasn't listening. "I wasn't going to lash myself down again either. But you get tired of dating. There ought to be a leash law for losers."

"It's a bad time for gadflies," I said. "Even if you don't catch anything you stand to lose your escort to the federal penitentiary system."

A pair of sad eyes got hard. "You wouldn't have heard that from anyone but Bill."

"We've met. That's what you've been trying to get me to admit, isn't it?"

"Then you *have* been following me. Or your partner has."

"I don't have a partner. Well, Detroit Edison. Is there a reason you should be followed?"

"That's what I most didn't like about the things I didn't like most about you," she said. "You never answered a ques-

65

tion with anything but another question. Okay, I lied when I said I just happened to look you up, but then you knew that. I—'' She sat back suddenly and busied herself with her drink.

Gail Hope, in her tight gown and Gidget make-up, leaned her profile next to mine. I hadn't heard her coming. ''Listen, I'm sorry,'' she said.

''That's okay. I like to watch the busboys earn their tips.''

''I don't mean the rotten table. Although I could do a lot better for you if you'd just call before coming. I mean about the wild goose chase with Sam Lucy. I didn't have any choice.''

''Forget it. You paid for the goose.''

''Well, the evening's on me. That'd be a start.'' She looked across at Catherine.

''My manners stink as usual,'' I said. ''Gail Hope, Catherine Sahara.''

''Sahara?'' Gail straightened. The room temperature dropped ten degrees.

''I had a hunch Bill didn't get around to introducing you. Gail's an old associate of your husband's,'' I told Catherine. ''She holds his cloak and dagger.''

She took in our hostess from hair to heels. ''He never told me. Are you with the government?''

''Not anymore,'' Gail said quickly. ''It's a pleasure, Mrs. Sahara. Welcome to the Canaveral.''

I finished my Scotch in the silence that followed. The empty glass caught Gail's eye.

''I'll send the girl over with another round,'' she said. ''If you need anything else, holler. Nobody goes home unhappy.'' She hung a smile on her face and left.

Catherine picked up her glass and held it to her chin. ''Gail Hope. Isn't that—?''

''Nice,'' I said. ''Everyone was nice in the sixties until the Beatles came. Why should anyone be following you?''

''I'm seeing someone. Bill knows, or suspects. I'm no spy, but I'm not blind.''

''What makes it he hired me?''

"I just said I'm stepping out on my husband. Don't you disapprove?"

"What makes it he hired me?"

She took a drink and set it down again. "Two of those thugs he sometimes works with came to the house one night. I don't sit in on Bill's meetings but I know a punk when I see one. I put their coats away. Your name and home address was written on a piece of paper in one of the pockets."

"But you're not a spy."

"I'm a wife. More of us ought to be spies. It comes naturally, or it did until some women only a blind man would ever propose to came along and liberated us. I checked the directory and found out you were still in the detective business."

The redhead delivered our second round and went away with my empty glass. The band was playing "Harbor Lights" in the tempo the Platters used, with a spangled ceiling globe casting scales of reflected light on the dancing couples. "Go again," I said. "A man in your husband's business might have a hundred good reasons to engage an investigator that wouldn't have anything to do with his domestic situation."

"I know when I'm being followed. Besides, I saw the man. That's why I thought you had a partner."

"What did you see?"

"A week ago I went to the dining room at the Westin to meet the man I've been seeing. I was early. I ordered coffee and got up to go to the ladies' room. The first thing you see when you open the door there is a mirror. He didn't get out of the way in time."

My inner smoke alarm had cut in. "What did he look like? Was he an older man, about sixty?"

"It was just a glimpse. He moved aside right away."

I took the picture Sahara had given me of Frank "Papa" Usher out of my wallet and laid it on her side of the table. "Use your imagination; this shot is thirty years old. Did he look anything like this?"

"Where did you get this?" She had studied it for only a moment.

"Is it him?"

"Of course not. This is a picture of Edgar Pym. The man I'm seeing."

12

"ARE YOU SURE?" I ASKED AFTER A MOMENT. "LOOK AGAIN.
The picture was taken a long time ago."

"He's white-haired now and his hair and face are thinner,
but that's Edgar. I've seen him very close up on several oc-
casions." Her expression went from arch to furious. "So
Bill does know. *Damn* being married to the government. He
has access to everything."

"I haven't been tailing you. He specifically told me to stay
away. What do you know about Edgar?"

"He's a retired history professor from a small college in
Alabama. His wife died last fall—they were married thirty-
eight years—and he moved here to be near friends. We met
at the A and P. In the frozen foods section, of course." She
tugged out the corners of her mouth in a way I remembered;
being sardonic for the balcony.

"I'll guess. He asked your opinion on how to thaw out a
TV dinner."

"Something like that. Oh, it was an obvious line. He was
so awkward about it I had to respond. Bill was away that
night. He so often is. We had dinner. In a restaurant. Edgar's
a warm and lonely man, and I'm just getting to an age where
I enjoy someone I can pretend to be a little girl with. I don't
understand this rage to go out with younger men. You get so

tired of sitting with your back to the light so your crow's-feet won't show.''

I didn't see any crow's-feet. When I knew her she'd had the largest assortment of oils and ointments on her night table this side of Madame Banzai's Tokyo Massage Emporium. "Did you check out his story?"

"Oh, of course. He was obviously just getting close to me so he could run off with last year's fox coat and my three-year-old Firebird with nine payments left on it. Why would an old man make up a boring past to impress me?"

"How long have you been seeing him?"

"You mean sleeping with him. About two weeks. It started a week after we met." She drank. "If that wasn't your man I saw in the mirror, who is he? And what's your business with Bill?"

The band had switched to a skull-rattling rendition of "House of the Rising Sun," complete with snarling basses and a psychedelic light show. I waited until it was over. "Do you know anything about your husband's work?"

"He sniffs out subversives in dangerous positions. As far as the neighbors are concerned he goes to the Federal Building every day, where he audits the books in some departments, but the truth is he can't balance a simple checkbook. I'm assuming you know all this. Otherwise I'm guilty of treason." She patted back an elaborate yawn.

"He says he's an assassin."

She gave it a beat. "He just came out and said that?"

"Well, counterassassin. Uncle Sam says attack and he rips out somebody's throat. He says."

"Bill doesn't even believe in hunting."

"Nobody pays you to go hunting."

"Do you believe him?"

"It isn't the kind of thing you lie about," I said. "He also says he wants out."

"I always thought he liked his work, whatever it was."

"It gets worse." I tapped the picture. "He gave me that. He thinks your Edgar has been sent after him by Washington

70

because they get nervous whenever a field man starts thinking about changing professions."

"Oh, please. *Bill* told you all this?"

"If what he really wants is to get me to scrape up evidence of your fling it's a bass-ackwards way of doing it, even for an employee of the government."

"What did he say he wanted you to do?"

"That's confidential."

"That's a crock."

"It makes a lot more sense if he's telling the truth," I said. "It would explain why Edgar—Sahara says his name is Frank Usher—sought you out, to keep tabs on your husband."

"Except he's never asked me anything about Bill."

"Didn't you wonder about that?"

"Maybe he's more interested in me," she said. "Maybe he'd rather spend time with me than leave me alone at home while he runs off to make the world safe for democracy. While we're talking about what makes sense, who the hell *is* following me and why?"

"Ask whoever it is who's following you."

"*You* ask him. He followed me here."

"Are you sure?"

"I told you I'm not blind. Don't ask me where he's sitting. I was too busy fighting with you from the moment we laid eyes on each other to notice."

"Let's forget him for now. Do you and Edgar talk about Bill?"

"As little as possible, and not nearly as much as I've told you, since you already know what he does. I don't mean kill people; I'll never buy that. A wife knows *something* about her husband. Remember?"

"If you did maybe we'd still be married. And maybe if I knew something about you, too. We sure made a muck of it."

"Water over the dam."

"Are you thinking of leaving Sahara?"

"I haven't gotten that far in my thinking. Why?"

71

"I was just going to tell you to wait."

"For what?" The hardness was back. "Is something going to happen?"

"Probably. It usually does. I'll tell you about it another time. Right now I want you to go to the ladies' room."

"What?"

"Take your purse."

She started to look around, stopped. Understanding set in. "What do I do when I get there?"

"That's up to you. Just take a long time doing it. Don't come out until I send word. I want him to think you crawled out a window or something."

She picked up her purse, a red leather item with a gold clasp, just big enough to hold a lipstick. "You won't make a scene."

"What do you care?"

"Same old Amos." She rose.

I stood politely. "Do you and Edgar Pym ever discuss literature?"

She tugged out the corners of her mouth. "You mean like *Fanny Hill*?"

"I mean like *The Voyage of Arthur Gordon Pym*, by Edgar Allan Poe. He also wrote 'The Fall of the House of Usher.' "

"That's pretty thin," she said after a moment.

I moved a shoulder. "Spies."

She went.

Alone, I sat back down and lit a Winston. I hadn't touched my second drink; I was on call. The redheaded carhop came over twice and I sent her away both times. The band played "It's My Party" and "Blue Moon." A few couples danced. The set ended. Some of the tables emptied. After a while the second wave came in, smelling of popcorn and talking animatedly about movies. The musicians mounted the platform again. He made his move then.

He jumped up from a table on the other side of the platform, almost knocking the table over. He caught it, tugged down his jacket with dignity, and started toward the rest rooms, skipping on every third step, trying not to run. He was a little guy with a pumpkin face and very fine blond hair over a pink scalp. He was wearing a green bow tie and a green-and-yellow houndstooth jacket that fit in at the Club Canaveral like a clown face at a funeral. I put out my cigarette and went after him. He was as hard to trail as Amtrak.

I walked down the narrow hallway paneled in cheap imitation wood with its framed stills from Gail Hope's pictures and two doors near the exit identified by cutout photographs of James Dean and Marilyn Monroe. The little guy in the noisy jacket was crouched with his ear to Marilyn's right breast. I went up and stood in front of him. His reaction when he saw my shoes was one for the album. He straightened quickly, almost butting my chin with the top of his head.

"Is this the men's room?" He was looking me square in the Adam's apple.

"The other one," I said. "The one without cleavage."

He mumbled thanks, stepped around me, and went through that door. I followed him in.

It was a small room, smelling of salt and lemons, with two urinals and two stalls and mirrored tiles over the pair of sinks. We were alone in it. A square speaker piped in "Dead Man's Curve" from the band platform. The little guy was washing his hands. I stood right behind him. He glanced up at our reflections, then down. He pumped sweet-smelling soap from the dispenser and scrubbed his knuckles and palms, rubbed it under his nails. They looked gnawed. He washed everything twice and took his time rinsing. He cranked two stiff brown paper towels out of the chrome container on the wall next to the sink and wiped his hands thoroughly. Not looking at anything. Finally he took a cheap red plastic comb out of his hip pocket, wet it under the faucet, and spent a few minutes carefully combing his thin blond hair, patting it down with his free hand. He had a doughy complexion, a small nothing of a nose, red lips, and long pale lashes. You could have traced his face around a pie tin.

A skinny kid of eighteen or so in a fatigue shirt and torn

73

jeans, with his hair in rolls of green and magenta, came in whistling "Dead Man's Curve," used one of the urinals loudly, and left without looking at us or washing his hands. While he was there, the little guy started to leave, but I poked a stiff finger into his back through my coat pocket and he stayed. I was unarmed that night; ex-wives hardly ever shoot.

When the kid left I poked the little guy again and checked him for weapons. He had none. I stepped back and frisked his wallet, a hand-tooled one like you find in souvenir shops, held together with a cowhide spiral. One driver's license made out to Herbert Selwyn Pingree. One snappy picture ID announcing that Herbert S. Pingree was licensed to practice private investigation in the State of Michigan. One friendly reminder from Herbert's dentist that he was scheduled for a cleaning next Tuesday at 3:00 P.M. Sixteen dollars in cash. I gave him back the wallet.

"You oughtn't to carry that much money around without a gun, Herbert. Or do you prefer Herb? It's my experience that men your size don't like to be called Herbie."

"What do you want?" He counted the bills and put the wallet away.

"For starters, why you're following Mrs. Sahara. Later we'll get around to who's paying you."

"Who are you?"

I showed him my ID. "It's not as new as yours."

The air went out of him then. He leaned back against the sink. "I must stink pretty bad."

"On ice, brother. Where'd you get your training?"

"I was a cop in Rouge for four years. I got tired of pulling skinny-dippers out of the river—the *Rouge*, for gosh sakes, it's a wonder they had any hide left—so I quit and hung out my shingle. Eight months ago it was. I guess I got a lot to learn."

"The lady spotted you right away. What's the action?"

"I'm just supposed to follow her, see where she goes and whom she meets and report back."

"Report back to who?"

"Whom." He actually blushed. "Sorry. My girlfriend
74

teaches fifth-grade English in Dearborn. I can't tell you the name of my client. That would be unethical.''

"Her husband, right?"

He said nothing.

The door started to open. "Out of order." I leaned it shut. "Herbert, Herbert. What are we going to do about this stalemate, Herbert?''

His face got a sly look. It was like watching Elmer Fudd coming up with a forty-watt idea. "Listen, I can use some help on this. You can't tail someone alone. I lost her twice already when I was in my heap because she found a parking space and I couldn't and I didn't have anyone to get out and shadow her on foot. Are you for hire?''

I looked at him for a long time. "I just had drinks with the lady. How do you know you're not offering a job to the other side?''

"If that's the case you'll turn me down. Anything else would be unethical.''

Someone on the other side of the door shoved hard and I almost fell down. I would almost have fallen down anyway. I put my back against it and braced my feet. "What kind of terms are we talking about?''

"Not here.'' Herbert S. Pingree took out his dentist's appointment card, clicked a ballpoint pen, and scribbled on the back. "This is my office address. Can you stop in tomorrow morning?'' He gave me the card.

I read the scrawl. "East Detroit?''

"Hey, if I could afford space anywhere else I could afford to have cards printed up, for gosh sakes. Can you make it?''

"Yeah.'' I stepped away from the door. He grabbed the handle. I grabbed his bow tie. It wasn't a clip-on. That was the first thing I'd found to admire about him; I never could tie one of the things. "If this is a dodge I'll push your face through the back of your head.''

He looked injured. "We're in the same line of work.''

I let him go, not gently. He tugged at the ends of his tie, patted his hair, jerked down his jacket, and went out around the line that was waiting to get inside.

75

A big shaven-headed black man in gold chains and a black caftan was the first one in. He glared at me with eyes that were pinpoints of gold in the shadow of his brow. "What's the deal?"

"AIDS inspection." I flashed the honorary sheriff's star pinned to my wallet. "This one looks clean."

The redhead in the carhop's uniform was emptying the ashtray at our table into a handheld scuttle with a lid. Catherine wasn't there. I'd forgotten about her. I put down money for the drinks, gave the redhead a ten, and asked her to tell the lady in the bathroom the coast was clear. The band was playing "Just Like Romeo and Juliet" when I left.

13

WARMTH WRAPPED ITSELF AROUND ME LIKE A HEATED towel when I opened the side door from the garage. My furnace was still working, even if the rest of my life wasn't. The oil stench got into the sandwich I made from the last edibles in the refrigerator, making it taste like something smoked over crude. I chased it with milk and poured myself a drink for dessert, but I felt lower than liquor could reach that night. I gave all but one sip a sea burial in the kitchen sink. It didn't go down. That night was the drain's turn.

When the plunger didn't do anything I stripped to the waist and took the trap apart with the big Johnny wrench that had come over from Brobdingnag with Gulliver. The plug of hair and black sludge that plopped out when I turned over the trap broke in two halves like an oyster shell, exposing my class ring, which I hadn't seen since June. I hoped it was a good omen.

It wasn't.

While I was wiping it with the rag I had under the sink, a pair of soft tasseled loafers walked up to the cabinet and stopped. I recognized the loafers. They were the next best thing to bare feet and therefore ideal for a trained kick-boxer like Bill Sahara's man Dan Wessell. I didn't see Earl Moss's box-toed Oxfords, but it was a fair bet they weren't far away. I needed a better lock on my front door.

I picked up the big wrench and brought the heavy end down as hard as I could on Wessell's right big toe. He howled and started dancing on the other foot. I swept the wrench sideways. It cracked against the raised bone of his left ankle and he made an animal noise and came down like a sack of doorknobs.

I scrambled out from under the sink. Earl Moss, standing by the door to the garage, was clawing a slim automatic out of a belt clip under his topcoat. I took two steps, almost tripping over his partner, and swung the wrench. The pistol went through the window over the little breakfast nook. I followed through, bending my elbow, and brought it up hard under his chin. His head snapped back, thumping the door. I backhanded and rammed the wrench handle into his groin. His eyes turned inward comically. He clutched himself with both hands and slid into a sitting position on the floor.

Wessell was rolling from side to side on the floor, clutching his smashed foot. I held the wrench ready while I groped inside his coat. He didn't object. A spring clip released his pistol into my hand, an L-frame Walther GSP .22 with a fourteen-shot magazine that fed through a rectangular extension of the trigger guard. The nub of exposed barrel was threaded for a suppressor.

A handsome gun, chalk-colored steel with a mutant grip shaped to snuggle into the fist. A light weapon, with almost no recoil and a report no louder than you'd make opening a pop bottle. A genteel killer, as common to the professional predators who prowl the airports and missile bases of the world as the tommy gun was to their grandfathers and the single-action Colt was to *their* grandfathers, who played faro with their off hands to keep their shooting hands free and called one another out into the street when they couldn't circle behind. It seemed a waste of modern technology on their class.

The telephone rang in the living room. I got rid of the wrench and went in and picked up the whole instrument and brought it to the kitchen door, which was as far as the cord would reach. I parked the pistol under my left arm to lift the receiver, then tucked the receiver under my chin and took the gun back in my right hand, supporting the telephone standard with my left.

"About time," I told the caller. "The boys were afraid you'd forgotten about them."

"Walker?" That arid voice, as empty of personality as a dial tone. "Put Moss on, I want to talk to him."

I looked at the big man, still holding himself and taking deep breaths and blowing them out. "He's indisposed. So's Wessell. Everyone's indisposed except me. May I take a message, Mr. Sahara?"

"What did you do to them?"

"Don't worry. Your place-kicker's on the disabled list for the season and you may have to change any plans you've made to put your fullback out to stud, but they're alive. Message, please."

"I told them to bring you to see me. I told them not to start anything."

"They started something when they walked into my house uninvited. I have a strong reaction to things like that. Especially after the same pair knocked me around in the concourse last week. Check the Michigan statutes on self-defense. Or is the law just something you smack when it lands on your cheek?"

"I want to see you."

"Make an appointment. You know my number at the office, also my shorts size." I cradled the receiver. The telephone began ringing again as I set it back down in the living room. I let it. Back in the kitchen, I nudged Moss with a toe. "Up, Rosencrantz. Take Guildenstern and dangle."

"What about our guns?" He worked the words up through his larynx like toothpaste through an exhausted tube.

"You'll get them back at the end of the semester. Let's move."

He put a palm on the floor and pried himself up, supporting his crotch with the other hand like a truss. "Jesus, I think I got a hernia."

"Next time wear a cup."

It was even money which man groaned loudest as Moss helped Wessell to his feet, or rather foot; the thinner man held up the crippled one like a lame stallion and leaned on his partner. The other leg wobbled. The ankle had begun to swell where I had struck it with the wrench, but it wasn't broken. I went ahead of them through the living room and held open the front door. On the stoop Moss paused. "I bet you think you're safe here."

"Safe's for the cemetery."

I watched from the doorway as they weaved down to the street. A light was on in the home of the Chrysler block assembly inspector who lived across from my house. *Two more damaged guests leaving the Walker place, Ruth. He must throw one hell of a party.*

After a while a car started up down the street and mumbled away. I got a flashlight then and went out and poked through the junipers under my kitchen window until I found Moss's pistol, another Walther GSP threaded for a suppressor. I put it along with Wessell's gun in my car so I wouldn't forget to take them to the office and found some cardboard to tack over the broken pane. Before I went to bed I added the window to the list of expenses in my notebook.

The telephone rang once again, but this time the caller gave up after six.

14

EAST DETROIT IS AN ANGRY CHILD, CONNECTED TO THE mother city by a steel umbilical cord and despising every inch of it. Bordered on the south by the Detroit leviathan, on the west by the sprawling General Motors playground of Warren, on the north by the essentially featureless Roseville, and on the east by the turquoise swimming pools, exclusive storefronts, and overcrowded berths of St. Clair Shores, it's a landlocked community that yearns to be an island and lacks only the business, industry, self-awareness, and courage to secede. Every generation or so it signs a petition to dump the Detroit from its name and votes against doing so. Of all of the city's dozens of boroughs, East Detroit alone refuses to accept its dependence as inevitable; but always in rhetoric, never at the polls.

That morning it was a November town, gray as rock mold and bleaker than Sunday in Toledo. A dusty snow had been falling since dawn, but the sidewalks and pavement were too warm to sustain it and the flakes sailed and spun like paper cinders on the ground currents and dissolved when they touched down. Pedestrians, what there were of them, hurried along with their hands in their coat pockets and their chins inside their collars, on the theory that wherever they were going had to be better than where they'd been. They weren't going where I was.

81

The address Herbert S. Pingree had given me belonged to a row of empty HUD houses off Gratiot with blank autistic windows and what remained of an office block constructed at the turn of the century, with faded brick fronts and iron fire escapes and on the east end squares of shredded wallpaper in different patterns and colors where the rest of the block had been torn away from a common wall; a crazy quilt of separate lives forgotten, like the silhouettes of vaporized victims burned into a wall in Hiroshima. I parked in a spot where I could watch the locals vandalizing my car from the windows and went inside.

The linoleum in the foyer, marbled with filth, peeled away from my heels when I lifted them. Most of the white plastic letters were missing from the wall directory. The elevator was vintage Otis with a cage and four dimples in the matted carpet made by the stool where the operator used to sit and work the handle before buttons were installed. That was a loss. I could have used a garrulous old man that morning with a weather eye for a hungover detective and a sure-fire cure. The car bellowsed and shuddered up the five stories to Pingree's floor, missing it by eight inches. I stepped out into a dim hall smelling of stale cigars and secondhand ideas. A building with character, the landlord would call it.

A hardwood floor in need of sanding and varnishing, plaster walls that had been patched and then touched up with paint a shade off the original. Anonymous offices dark behind their beveled glass panels. Spotty legends on doors flanked by vacant rooms: APEX DENTAL SUPPLY; BARLOW GREGG, ATTORNEY AT LAW; PEERLESS VIDEOS; KARL'S KAR-AVAN OF KOMIX; UNIQUE NAILS AND ELECTROLYSIS. The sad monotonous gauntlet of Zeniths, A-1s, and Acmes that collect at the nadir of capitalism like flotsam in a storm drain. If they advertised at all it was after the Japanese movie between the midnight party line and Wazoo Waterbeds. Someone had a TV set tuned to a manic local talk show, entertaining himself between customers. Someone else, similarly unencumbered, yawned bitterly, squeaked his desk chair, and yawned again. Behind Barlow Gregg's door a hunt-and-

82

pecker plucked without enthusiasm at a manual keyboard, polishing a tort or writing a letter to the landlord in lieu of that month's rent while his secretary was out filing a claim against her employer for back wages. A story in back of every lettered window, a little tragedy with all the raw dramatic power of a notice under Situations Wanted. An office whose shadow haunted the nightmares of slipping account executives and middle-aging vice presidents with young sharks working just below them. A roof and four walls between the occupant and the line where they gave out surplus food. Chapter Eleven and a Half.

The number I wanted was part of a two-room suite, intended originally as an office and a reception room, one to let the public in, the other to let the busy executive out in case he didn't like the looks of the public. Now they belonged to two separate businesses. The door on the private office, a corner room, read ANTOINETTE'S ACADEMY OF MASSAGE. The other announced itself as the portal to TRANS-GLOBAL INVESTIGATIONS, painted in an impressive arch with *"Herbert S. Pingree, President"* closing it off in smaller letters at the bottom. Inside the arch, straddling a gridded globe, was a pair of stylized eyes, twice as many as Pinkerton's. They seemed to be looking down the hall for bill collectors.

I raised my fist to knock, stopped. On the other side of the door something shattered that was made of glass. It was followed by a noise I was more familiar with than I wanted to be, a kind of crumpling thud coupled with a grunt.

I was heeled that morning. I drew the Smith & Wesson and held it barrel high as I twisted the doorknob, leaning my weight on it so it wouldn't rattle. It rotated without resistance and I went in with the door, bringing the revolver down and my other hand up off the knob to support my wrist, just like on the range. That gave me the drop on an uninhabited office.

It was half again deeper than a closet, but not much wider: If you stretched your arms out sideways you could almost touch both side walls. They had been painted recently, a deep forest green to cover the inevitable mustard yellow. The dark color made the room seem even smaller. A crisp new investigator's license hung next to the door in a drugstore frame. Behind an imitation woodgrain desk, a window with its shade drawn halfway down looked out on a laundromat and a speedy printer's. An old-fashioned water cooler burped in a corner and I almost shot it. There was a good walnut four-shelf bookcase stuffed with yellow law books and a set of blue numbered volumes on forensic science that I recognized. I received a flyer a couple of times a year asking me to subscribe to the series; they threw in the one on finger-printing free when you placed your order. It looked like Herbert had a complete set.

A curved shard of thick transparent glass winked at me from under the window, between the edge of the beige rug and the baseboard. It belonged to a tumbler. The hand that had held it—or maybe it wasn't the hand—was clutching the edge of the desk on the far side. The nails looked gnawed. I stepped closer.

He was down on one knee, wedged between the chair and the desk, with his other leg stretched out inside the kneehole. He had on the same green-and-yellow jacket or one like it. There couldn't be another one like it. Holstering the .38 I went around the desk and eased back the chair. Herbert S. Pingree unfolded himself and sagged onto his back on the floor. As I bent over him, I heard the rattle and wheeze of the elevator down the hall. I straightened quickly, taking the gun out again, and reached the hall in three strides, but the indicator over the cage had already slid down to two. I put away the .38 and went back inside.

Kneeling with my ear to Pingree's chest, I thought I heard a heartbeat. Then I thought it was mine. I plucked some fibers from the carpet and held them under his nostrils. They seemed to be stirring, but I couldn't tell if it was because he was still breathing faintly or because of the drafts that lanced through the rickety old building like a magician's knives. I took off my coat and bunched it under his shoulders, tipped back his head, pinched his nose, gulped air, and breathed into his mouth. I kept that up for five minutes. Then I put my ear to his chest again. There was nothing going on there. I felt the big artery on the side of his neck. I stood up.

The base of the broken glass had come to rest rightside up on the carpet. There was some clear liquid in the bottom. I picked it up with my handkerchief and stuck my nose inside. A scorched, bitter smell. You'd think he'd have noticed it. Maybe he didn't want to seem impolite. I put the base down where I'd found it.

The desk contained a blotter and pen set with matching brass trim, aside from the bookcase the single largest investment in the room. Probably an office-warming gift. A red plastic frame that went like hell with the set contained a portrait, one shoulder turned mock-seductively toward the camera, of a honey blonde with slightly protruberant blue eyes, a large nose, and an overbite. The hair was her best feature, but I liked the face fine. Nobody had been at it with a mallet and scalpel and a picture of Linda Evans for a model.

Pingree's appointment book was blank but for a single note on the top page: "Lunch Edie, Black Bull, 12:30." It didn't look like any sort of code. I tore off the page and pocketed it.

I went through the drawers. Scissors, rubber bands, envelopes, a copper letter-opener with a lion's head for a handle. Desk stuff. A collection of paperback detective novels in the deep file drawer, thumb-blurred and bloated. Herbert would sit with his feet crossed on the desk, reading and waiting for an exotic woman with a thick accent to come swaying through the door and offer to fall in love with him if he found her emerald necklace. While he was waiting he would have lunch with Edie of the Incisors. No telephone or address book. Herbert would have no addresses or telephone numbers to put in it except Edie's, and he would have that memorized. He'd mentioned a girlfriend who taught English in Dearborn. The honey blonde looked like a teacher. I didn't know what teachers looked like these days. I was just playing detective.

There was a side door that would connect with Antoinette's Academy of Massage, the other office in the suite. I tried it. Locked. A radio was playing easy listening music very low on the other side. I used my handkerchief on the things I'd touched in the office and went outside and rapped on Antoinette's door. A female voice invited me in.

It was a corner room as I said, twice as big as Pingree's, painted dark red, with two windows on adjoining walls. A sort of cubicle had been constructed out of partitions to the left of the door with an archway closed off by wine-colored velvet curtains. Matching hangings draped the walls like bunting. A pile carpet the color of intestinal blood tickled my ankles. The music was muted and the place smelled of incense and liniment and more delicate oils in pump containers on shelves in back. She came to me from that direction, a small brown girl with her dark hair in a straight page-boy that may have been a wig and a silver-blue robe knotted around her waist with a green sash. Her bare feet were in platform sandals. I had a hunch I was looking at everything she had on. The hunch was confirmed when she passed through a shaft of weak sunlight and for a brief moment the robe became transparent. Her smile looked natural enough until you saw her eyes.

"Are you Antoinette?" I asked.

"No, I'm Cathay. Like in Cathy, only with an extra *a*." Her voice said it was the first time the question had ever been asked. Her eyes added another digit to an invisible scoreboard.

"Cathay, you don't look Chinese."

"It's okay. Antoinette isn't French." The smile faltered as she stopped in front of me, then came back with a determined kind of energy.

My jaw ached. I realized I was grinning like a skull. I pulled my lips down over my teeth with an effort. Anybody not in Cathay's racket would have run for cover at the sight of me. "How long have you been here, Cathay?"

"About a year. The massage will be fifty dollars. You can take your clothes off in there." She indicated the curtained cubicle.

"I don't want a massage. I didn't mean how long you've

86

been working here. I'm not making conversation. I meant how long have you been here today?''

The smile shut down permanently. An essentially grave young black woman had been standing behind it, showing tiny lines in her face that should not have been there at her age, or what I judged her age to be. I gave her a quick look at the sheriff's buzzer. She looked tired suddenly. "I'm a licensed massage therapist," she said. "You can't bust me for that."

"Relax. I'm interested in your neighbor, the sleuth."

"Sleuth?"

"Shamus. Gumshoe. Hawkshaw. Peeper. I'd say dick, but it probably wouldn't mean the same thing in the massage business." She was still in the dark. I said, "The private detective. Next door? That's the thing with the knob on it down the hall. Stop me when it sounds like English."

"Oh, Herbie. We haven't had any trouble with him since we made him patch up the hole. Did he drill one on the other side?" A forehead line deepened. "Wait a minute, that's the comic book place. You better show me that badge again. It didn't look like no city shield." Her grammar was slipping.

"Why bother? It's just a gag. I'm private too. I just want to ask if you saw or heard who visited him today."

"Why?"

I got out the wallet again and gave her fifty of William Sahara's dollars. "Tell Antoinette you had a customer. Or don't tell her and buy yourself some underwear. The person I'm interested in just left."

She put the bills in a pocket of her robe. "You might as well take your clothes off, mister. You wasted your money otherwise. I didn't hear nothing. I had the radio on since I got in."

"I heard it in Herbie's office. The walls in this dump are made of tissue paper and trust. You must have heard something. Voices, a glass breaking."

"Why ask me, if you were in there? Ask Herbie. Oh." It dawned on her then. She looked a little sad, as if her favorite soap opera had been pre-empted. "I heard two guys talking.

87

Herbie was one of them. I didn't hear any words. It didn't sound like nobody was mad or nothing. What happened, he get cut?''

"He got poisoned. I think."

"Jesus. Was it in his water?''

"Looks like it. Did he drink a lot of water?''

She nodded. "He had a fresh bottle delivered every couple of weeks. The customers sure weren't drinking it. Herbie didn't have no customers.''

"Sounds like you know a lot about him.''

"Like you said, these walls are a joke. Also we saw each other in the hall. He liked to talk. Did you know he was a direct descendant of the Mayor Pingree that turned the vacant lots in Detroit into potato patches to feed the poor?''

"He never told me. Did he talk about the case he was working on?''

"I didn't know he was working at all. Today was the first time I heard anyone in there with him in weeks. Well, except the bottled water man. Hey, maybe he's the one put in the poison.''

"When was the last delivery?''

She thought. "A week ago, about.''

"If it was in the bottle he'd be dead a week.''

"Maybe it, like, built up in his system.''

"Cyanide doesn't work that way. That's what I smelled in his glass.''

Her eyes opened a little. They looked like the eyes on the door of Trans-Global Investigations. "Cyanide, that's heavy. Ain't it hard to get hold of?''

"Ask me questions when the fifty bucks is used up. What was the other man's voice like? Deep? High? Gruff? Did he sound like he operated a power shovel or danced the Carioca for his living?''

"It was kind of medium, I think. I didn't pay much attention. I was listening to the radio.'' She glanced at a tiny watch on her wrist. "I got a regular coming in at ten. He don't like it when somebody else is here.''

"Tell the councilman to wait in the Omar Sharif Room.

The building's going to be crawling with cops in a little while. Where did Herbie live?''

"With his girlfriend. If he told me that once he told me a hundred times. I think she was his first. That boy was pussy-whipped.''

"That'd be Edie? Where's she live?''

"We didn't exchange addresses. Her name's Hubbard. No, Hibbard. Edith Hibbard. Can't be far. Herbie used to go home for lunch, and maybe a quickie. Something tells me quickies were all anybody ever had with Herbie.''

I wrote the name in my notebook. "I'd better use your telephone to call the cops. They get awful upset when you smear up the one at the murder scene.''

"How come all the shit happens when I'm in charge?'' she said.

I took the receiver off a maroon wall unit and punched buttons. "I was going to ask the same question.''

15

THERE IS A PATTERN TO THESE THINGS, AS IMMUTABLE AND unvarying as a bride's first meal followed by a groom's first heartburn: The uniforms arrive first, then the plainclothes detectives. It's one of the Unwritten Laws, a penal code that would run to several hundred volumes if anyone ever chose to set it down. In East Detroit on the day Herbert Selwyn Pingree drank his last glass of water, they came together. You could call it a refreshing example of democracy in practice. You could call it plain dumb coincidence and be right. I didn't think they were pooling, but you never knew what elected officials would come up with next in an economic crunch that was approaching drinking age.

While the uniforms went about their business of dispersing the street crowds they had gathered in the first place with their pretty lights and sirens, a Sergeant Trilby shook my hand and steered me into a vacant office down the hall for a chat. It was a square empty room with a painted steel radiator and the inescapable mushroom-shaped glass fixture suspended upside-down from the ceiling, suitable for snaring dust and expired flies. The walls and ceiling were painted the original sickly yellow and a window with a slanted shade offered a view of an abandoned Pinto in an empty lot.

"You like November?" Trilby asked me.

"I used to, when I hunted deer."

"Why'd you stop?"

"It reminded me of some things."

"Yeah, I saw that movie too." He dusted his palms, indicating that the small talk was over. Trilby was youngish, with black hair cut short and combed down over a slightly low forehead like Jack Kennedy's, dark, intelligent eyes—no cops' rude, weary-of-the-human-race stare there; not yet, anyway—and a pug nose that contributed to his youthful appearance. I wasn't sure if he really was young or if I was just getting old. I decided he really was young. I needed a break.

He consulted an alligator-hide notebook. "You told the officers you had an appointment with this Pingtree?"

"Pingree," I corrected. "It wasn't really an appointment. He asked me to come up when I got a chance."

"Had you known each other long?"

"About fifteen minutes total, not counting artificial respiration."

"What was he to you, if not a friend?"

"A guy in the same racket. I ran into him last night in the Club Canaveral. He found out I was in the business and he wanted to talk about partnering. He said the case he was on needed two men."

"What was the case?"

"He didn't say."

Trilby frowned at his notebook. He didn't like what he was writing. I didn't care for it much myself. "I'm not clear on how it is you happened to run into each other last night."

"He was tailing someone. He might have been more obvious about it if they'd put him under the main spot and vamped him, but I doubt it. I braced him and treated him to a little free advice, one P.I. to another."

"Generous of you."

"I get that way when I'm drinking."

"Who was he tailing?"

"A woman. I'd have paid more attention to her if Pingree weren't more entertaining. He almost followed her into the toilet."

He changed directions. "It says here you heard the killer

escape in the elevator while you were busy with Pingree. What makes you think it was him—or her? Poisoning's a woman's game.''

"Not since liberation. Cyanide works quick, within minutes of ingestion. I figure whoever put it in Pingree's glass waited to see him drink it before he left. *I* would if it were me and I went to that much trouble. I got to Pingree's door in time to hear the glass drop from his hand when he collapsed. Nobody used the elevator before that except me. There's no access to the stairs from this floor. I checked.''

"There's always the fire escape.''

"He'd have to pass too many windows on his way down. Someone would see him. The way I take it, when he heard me coming up in the elevator he ducked into a vacant office, maybe this one, and waited until I went into Pingree's.''

"You make him sound like a pro.''

"Pro enough anyway to slip a private cop a Mickey when everyone else out there is gun happy. This guy likes his work or he wouldn't be into the refinements.''

"I don't like poison," Trilby said. "I don't like it because I don't come across it. I'm used to punks plugging each other over a noseful of crack, a wife slipping her old man the butcher knife when he's hitting her with the rest of the kitchen. Most of the time the perp's still standing there holding the weapon when the uniforms come. Poison's for dowagers who go to garden parties to gossip about the vicar.'' He looked at his notebook one more time, shook his short-cropped head, and flipped down the cover. "No, I don't like poison.''

Nothing there had my name on it, so I let it go. He put away the notebook and glanced at my suit, in a way that made his interest look no more than curious. No conflict there: Together we wouldn't dress out to three hundred dollars. His was a three-button Ivy Leaguer that had seen better days and would probably see a lot worse before he got rid of it, under a cream-colored car coat with a pile collar. He looked like a diffident fraternity brat, carefully mussed. "What were you doing in the Club Canaveral?''

"Meeting a woman.''

"Named?"

"You wouldn't know her."

"It's going to be like that, is it?"

"It doesn't have to be," I said. "She's got nothing to do with this. It was just an accident Pingree and I met."

"I don't like accidents much more than I like poison. Whenever something new comes into a man's life—you, in this case—and the man winds up not having that life soon after, I have to jump on the something new. There's nothing personal in it; I've got a friend on the department who moonlights as a private investigator and I let him in my front door and everything. It's just a question of averages." He changed tack again. "That was a good call on the cyanide. It'll be even better if the coroner says that's what did it. How come you know so much about it?"

"I went to detective class."

He was silent for a moment. "I don't need a citizen soldier from Detroit coming up here telling me I'm stupid, but I can live with it. What I can't live with is one coming up here *thinking* I'm stupid."

"You're right. Sorry, Sergeant." I shook a quarter-inch of Winston out of a new pack and offered it to him. He turned it down. I pulled it the rest of the way out with my lips and lit it. I stepped on the match. "Kissing a corpse isn't the way I like to start most days. Besides, I kind of liked the little guy. He was like a clumsy puppy you want to pick up and take home before he gets gassed."

"What I'm having trouble buying is that a P.I., *any* P.I., would just up and offer to go partners on fifteen minutes' acquaintance."

"Pingree wasn't any P.I. He was as new as a baby tooth and didn't know the business from the leading brand. You saw the books in his desk drawer. He thought it was all blondes and midnight meetings on the riverfront and when he found out it wasn't, he got confused. When I came along he snatched at me like a piece of driftwood. I imagine he was looking for pointers."

"And you just ate it up."

"I don't get asked for advice that often. Besides—"

"You liked the little guy. Okay, Walker." He opened the door and held it. "Stick around the area in case we need a statement." When I started to go through, he touched my arm, not threateningly. "This isn't Detroit. We haven't gotten around to considering murder a natural cause. If we don't turn something in seventy-two hours we go back to the starting line. You'll be doing yourself a favor if we don't have to come looking for you then. I'm not nearly as nice as I seem the first time you meet me. Ask my brother-in-law."

"That's clear enough," I said.

"I'm glad. Everyone likes to be understood."

There was a bar around the corner, a little black cavity of a place with four stools at the bar and a row of booths in back. The bartender was young and fair, with a sprouting of reddish moustache. Everybody I met lately was young. I wondered if there had been a coup while I was busy rocking and thinking about my shuffleboard game. I ordered bourbon straight up.

He set it and a paper napkin in front of me. "Nothing like that first shot to jump-start your heart in the morning," he said. "You look like your battery's low."

"When I want a shrink I'll go the yard an hour. I came in here for sunshine in a glass."

"Excuse me, Pete. I'm just the help. The observations are free. Sunshine's a buck seventy-five."

I grunted, put down two singles, took my change, and went over to the pay telephone at the end of the bar. I dialed my answering service.

"A woman called twice, Mr. Walker. She said her name was Catherine. She sounded upset."

"You'd be too if somebody left you in a toilet."

"I'm sorry?"

"Just saying something cryptic under my breath so I'll sound wise and weary. Anybody else?"

She said no. Well, Sahara preferred to make his visits in person. I hung up, forgetting to thank her, and returned to my stool. The whiskey tasted better than expected, better than I wanted it to at that hour. I looked at my watch to see what hour it was. Eleven thirty-eight. Pingree had a lunch date at 12:30. "Ever hear of a restaurant called the Black Bull?" I asked the bartender.

"Now I'm the auto club."

"Direct hit." I nodded. "So far the day's a stinkeroo and I don't have a wife or a dog. Maybe you've had days like that."

He slapped his rag at the beer pulls. "Maybe I have."

"I'll start fresh if you will."

He put away the rag, touched his moustache. "It's a steak place down on Eight Mile, the Detroit side I think. I hear they serve a mean prime rib."

"You don't know?"

"I'm a vegetarian."

"You're kidding."

"Would I kid about a thing like that?"

"Hitler probably wouldn't either. He was a vegetarian too."

"Yeah? I wonder if it gave him gas like it does me. That could explain Poland."

"What's a youngster like you know about Hitler and Poland?"

"Plenty. My folks are from Warsaw."

I appreciated that for a moment. "What do you know about a guy named Hazen S. Pingree?"

"He doesn't sound Polish."

"He wasn't. A long time ago he planted potatoes to feed the poor. He ran for governor."

"I bet he lost."

"It was a gentler time," I said. "People were more compassionate. He lost by a landslide."

"Was he a vegetarian?"

"I don't know. Does it matter?"

"Probably not." He unbuttoned his cuffs and turned them back. The room was a little overheated, as bars are everywhere when it's cold out. "I can't help wondering how many of those spuds made it to the poor."

I tipped him a buck and slid off the stool. "Buy yourself a rutabaga."

"Anything wrong with the drink?" I hadn't touched it after the first sip.

"Nothing. I wanted there to be, but there isn't. That's what's wrong."

"The Bull doesn't open till noon," he said. "Where you planning to wait?"

I pushed the door open two inches and stopped. A tall narrow wedge of clammy air touched me from hat to heels. "There's got to be a Christian Science reading room somewhere in this town."

"Lots of luck, pal." He dumped my bourbon into the sink behind the bar and washed the glass.

16

WHAT I DID WAS DRIVE.

When they were stumped in ancient Greece, they went to the oracle at Delphi. At Lourdes they take the waters, and I suppose in Akron they go down and watch the tires being made. In Detroit, where we put the world on wheels, or did anyway until the Japanese and the Yugoslavs and the Brits rolled in, when our brains slip into neutral we lay rubber on the road and hit the gas.

I had been driving my antebellum Mercury for several months, ever since my Chevy Cavalier had been shot to pieces, a hard thing to collect insurance on, especially when you leave it unlocked and unattended in the warehouse district after dark. The Merc was one of the old square four-barrel dinosaurs, slab-sided and bigger than Lake Superior, with an unslakable thirst for high-test leaded and 10-W-40. Driving the Chevy I hadn't realized how much I missed carburetors, the dub-dub-dub of a big engine at idle or the feeling, when you press the pedal to the firewall, that you've left the chains of gravity behind and are shrieking into deep space. I took Gratiot clear down to McNichols and McNichols to Outer Drive, the old Detroit city limits before the developers acquired their bottomless hunger for parks and farmland and began a fifteen-mile-wide crawl northward, devouring trees and grass as they went and dropping concrete and asphalt behind them like manure. I passed subdivisions and 7-Elevens, HUD houses that had never been lived in and doorways that were, schools and factories and family practice clinics and the great expanse of Mt. Olivet Cemetery, yawning on both sides of the road and studded with granite angels and gunsight crosses and American Legion flags and family plots occupied by the aged dead and their seventeen-year-old grandchildren, shot down in the hallways and on the steps of local high schools by other seventeen-year-olds because somebody had refused to lend somebody else his notes from Social Sciences. I passed great olive UPS trucks and low slinky Firebirds, city blue-and-whites and rusty puckered heaps with their radios cranked up all the way, as if the cars ran purely on the brain-thudding banality of Rap. I nicked red lights and powered through amber. I was engaged in an eight-cylinder voyage in search of the golden fleece of logic.

The Herbert S. Pingrees of this world aren't supposed to wind up murdered. They're charted for public-school educations, two years of business college, marriage to a plump girl who in middle age will starve and exercise herself down to gristle, tint her hair the ubiquitous beige, and complain that they never go anywhere. The Herbert S. Pingrees of this world are down for three children, one of them a problem, early hair loss, office football pools, and retirement in a concrete bungalow in Florida where the kids never visit. When they die, it's supposed to be from too many potato chips and Sunday roasts and beers with the Five O'Clock Club on the way home from work. Nobody is supposed to find them crumpled up with a bellyful of cyanide in a cardboard office in East Detroit between a rub-a-dub emporium and Lawyer Dan, the Ambulance Man. A Teflon drawer in the county deep freeze is no place for the Herbert S. Pingrees of this world.

Damn him anyway for snarling the statistics. I wasn't in business to lie to the cops for Pingrees.

At Conant I turned around and drove back the way I'd come, faster this time. The lights were all going to have to be with me if I were to keep a date for a dead man. He'd screwed me up again, making me forget to check my watch.

The restaurant wasn't hard to find for an experienced detective. It was a low sprawling red-brick building in the center of an asphalt parking lot with its name on a free-standing electric sign forty feet high and a black bull on its roof. A kid could have used the ring in its nose for a hula hoop.

Inside, the motif was country kitchen. The floor was laid in sheets of broad planking with imitation pegs, the tables looked like butcher blocks, and homely samplers lined the printed-paper walls. The waiters were all in their twenties and wore white aprons that covered them from neck to knees. Knives and forks clattered, people talked like dogs barking in a kennel. It was a popular place.

Edie was seated facing the door in a booth near the back. She wore a pink mock-turtleneck sweater and silver hoops in her ears, and her dark blond hair was pulled back and tied loosely behind her neck. The hair looked even better than in her photograph, waving naturally from a not-too-severe part in the center and gleaming softly and deeply, like cognac. She would wash it nightly in an herbal shampoo and stroke it one hundred times with a brush with natural bristles, applying the same kind of gratitude and awe that a poor man brings to his only valuable possession. As I approached the booth, she checked the time on a silver watch pinned above her left breast, made to look like a miniature grandfather's clock complete with a pendulum that never moved; and I knew then with as much certainty as I knew anything that she still had the dollhouse her parents had given her for her eighth birthday, adding to it from time to time.

"Edith Hibbard?"

She looked up, startled. In person as in her picture, her blue eyes stood out a little, but they had a luminous effect, as in an Elizabethan painting. Her upper lip didn't quite cover her prominent front teeth. "Yes?"

"I'm Amos Walker, a friend of Herb's. He asked me to meet you. He's going to be a little late." I held out one of my cards.

She took it and read it. "He never mentioned you. Are you working together on something?"

"Sort of. May I sit down?"

"I guess so." She laid the card facedown next to her silverware.

I pegged my coat and hat on a partition between booths and slid in opposite her. The dividers extended eight inches above the red vinyl upholstery, creating the illusion of private rooms.

She tried a smile that made me think of a pep rally. "Herbert never talks about his work. I think he thinks I don't approve of it."

"Do you?"

"I don't really understand it. My father offered him a job in the cement plant he manages, a desk position, but he turned it down. Herbert says he wants to make his own way."

"There's something to be said for that." It sounded like an epitaph.

"Maybe. If only he weren't in that awful building."

"He hasn't been spending his allowance next door, if that's what you're worried about."

"Next door? Oh." She colored. You can't fake that. She was younger than she looked in her picture, in her late twenties. For all that she didn't seem as young as Pingree. Women straddle that line more often than men.

"That's a nice desk set you bought Herb," I said.

"Oh, did he tell you I gave it to him?"

"He didn't get around to it. It looked like a woman's taste."

"Which is?"

"Better than mine."

A waiter came. Edie asked for a glass of water. I ordered coffee. When we were alone again: "You said Herb never discusses his work. Does he keep records?"

"I don't know. He has a desk at home he keeps locked. Why don't you ask him?"

"He's pretty busy."

It sounded lame as hell, but she didn't seem to be paying

much attention. The waiter returned, set a tall amber glass of water in front of her, and filled the cup at my elbow from a carafe. She waited until he left. "It really doesn't matter," she said. "About the massage place, I mean. Didn't Herbert tell you? He's moving out soon."

"Of his building?"

"No, out of the apartment. Our apartment. Well, my apartment; Herbert barely makes enough to keep up the rent on the office. I've met someone."

I don't know why it rocked me. It wasn't shaping up to be one of Herbert's better days. "Did you tell him?"

She sat back then, her antennae fully extended. "Maybe I shouldn't be telling *you*. I've only known you five minutes."

"You didn't tell him."

"We discussed his moving out. I told him I thought it was a good idea. I said we needed some time apart. If that isn't telling him, what is?"

"Telling him," I said. "Herb's grasp of the obvious is slippery at best."

Her eyes had a hurt-deer look. "Why are you so angry? I was right, I shouldn't be telling you any of this." She glanced down at the tiny grandfather's clock on her bosom. "Did Herbert say how late he was going to be? I have to be back at school in an hour."

I stood up. "I just remembered I have to make a telephone call."

I walked past the pay telephone and through an arch to the rest rooms. In the men's room I grasped the sink with both hands and looked at my reflection in the mirror. It was my face, all right. I recognized the sly cast of the features, the feral gleam in the eyes, the predatory mouth. Someone with a face like that would crank up a dead man and make him walk around one more time, just long enough to turn out his pockets and count his valuables. He would rob graves, con widows, and rip the DO NOT REMOVE tags off mattresses. Nothing was beyond him, least of all lying to Snow White

101

about the state of Dopey's health to find out what he could about Dopey's last days.

Sweet women lie, kid, Dale Leopold had said, a long time ago, when he found out his partner was going to be married. *Men lie to get something or get out of something. Women lie because they're good at it. The sweeter the woman, the better the liar. They're so good at it they hardly ever have to pull a trigger. Somebody always does it for them.* As good a liar as Catherine was she had nothing on Edie. Pingree had gone to the morgue thinking she was still his. But lying to her didn't square anything.

Dale was dead, too. Over a woman. She hadn't even been in the same zip code when the trigger was pulled.

I dashed water in my face and mopped it dry with paper towels. It was just a face after all, no better than most and not as good as some, but the one I had to look at if I didn't want to go through life tripping over my beard. I ran a comb through my hair, straightened my tie, lifting the knot away from the shirt the way they advised in *GQ*, and went back and sat down opposite Edie. She was reading the menu now.

"He's dead," I said.

She looked at me over the top of the menu. "Who is?"

"Herbert. Last time I saw him the cops were tracing him with masking tape on the carpet in his office."

"How—?" It didn't mean anything yet. She was just asking the questions you ask when you don't understand any of the answers.

"Murdered. Poisoned, to put the fine point on it. This morning. Someone put cyanide in the water he's always drinking. Or something that smelled a lot like cyanide and worked just as thoroughly."

"My Herbert?"

"I tried CPR. Potassium cyanide paralyzes the breathing muscles; that's how it works. If you get to them quick enough and can keep forcing air into their lungs until the paralysis wears off, you can save them. I didn't get to him quick enough." I paused. "If it means anything, I don't think he suffered much. It's a fast poison."

102

"If it means anything."

There was no hysteria, just a lot of quiet tears. The diners seated near us didn't even look around. I saw our waiter coming and waved him away. I went for my handkerchief, but I wasn't fast enough. Again. She opened a burlap purse with a daisy embroidered on it and took out some Kleenexes. I sipped coffee while she made repairs. It had grown cold, but not as cold as Herbert.

She closed the purse with a sharp snap. Her face was flushed, but it might have been from the November air outside if you hadn't seen her crying. "Who?"

"That's the question the police are asking. They'll get around to asking you after they finish talking to a girl named Cathay. You're sure Herb never told you what he was working on?"

"If you were his partner, you'd know. Who are you?"

"The card I gave you is genuine. Herb and I were in the same business and that's as much as I knew about him until this morning when I found him." I told her about the Club Canaveral, as much of it as I'd told Sergeant Trilby. "If I'm going to find out what his death has to do with anything, I'll need to know who hired him and why. You said he kept a locked desk at home. Can I look inside it?"

"Why should I let you?"

"No reason. I don't know much about the cops in East Detroit, but I know cops, and the smallest police force in the world is better equipped to handle murder than I am. On the other hand, if what I suspect draws any water, I may be holding more threads in this tangle than anyone else, and maybe one man can follow them farther faster than any local bureaucracy. In any case we'll all have the same chance; a detective sergeant who calls himself Trilby and looks like something on the other end of a Phi Beta Kappa key will be calling on you any time." I shut up for a beat. What the hell, cue the strings. "Besides, maybe Herbert would prefer I had a hand in."

That surprised her. "Why would he? You just said you never met before last night."

103

"Look at it from his side. If he was like the rest of us who ever shared housekeeping with a woman, he spent a good deal of time trying to make you approve of what he did. That desk set was a good move on your part, but he'd need more. If a fellow P.I. were to help clear up his murder, he might feel vindicated in his career choice. Call it one last gift from you and me, in place of what he should have gotten when he was here to appreciate it."

A busboy cruised over carrying a pitcher of water, saw that Edie's hadn't been touched, and sailed off. She ignored him. "Does that approach work very often?"

"Almost never." I sighed, sitting back. "Herb would've eaten it up."

"That's the first thing you've said I agree with." She slid to the edge of the booth. "Will you excuse me?"

"Back to school, huh?"

"No, I have to make a call. They'll need to find a substitute for my afternoon classes. The apartment's in Dearborn. Can you follow me that far, or do all detectives get lost as easily as Herbert?"

17

THE APARTMENT WAS IN A NEW BRICK COMPLEX OFF SCHAF-fer, set back two hundred feet from the highway at the end of a private street with a parking lot in front and a deer park behind, where the residents could stand on their narrow balconies and watch the tough city squirrels mugging each other for acorns. Dearborn was built by Ford for Ford. Its citizens drive Fords. Henry the First put together his prototype buggy there in a brick shed behind his house in 1896. Twelve years later he stamped his name all over the city, just as he did with his beloved Model T, and to this day you can drive there by way of Ford Road past Fordson High School, enter the Edsel Ford Freeway, and pass the Ford River Rouge plant. In 1914, Ford's production line flooded Detroit with black immigrants looking for work, changing the complexion of the city forever, but not so many years ago a black family couldn't live in Dearborn without having bricks thrown through their windows on a daily basis.

We parked a few spaces apart—true to her community, Edie drove a two-year-old white Escort—and she unlocked a glass security door and led me up a quiet flight of shag-carpeted steps to the second floor, where the apartment she had shared with Pingree faced the parking lot. The layout was L-shaped, with a combined kitchen and living room taking up the shaft of the L and a small bedroom and bath in the leg. A sliding glass door opened onto a balcony where one person could stand comfortably. A brown mohair sofa and two matching chairs shared the living room with a console color TV, some magazines, a midget rolltop desk, and good Impressionist prints on the walls. There was a double bed in the bedroom between matching nightstands with pottery lamps on them and a Maxfield Parrish poster mounted over the headboard, showing a square-rigger heeling through a storm of whitecaps and orange lightning. I thought I could guess who had picked out the art in which room.

Edit took my coat and hat and hung them with her coat in a closet. I wandered over to the little rolltop. "This the one?"

"Yes. I don't have a key. Can you pick a lock?"

I grasped the top and pulled. It rolled up without resistance.

"It's always been locked before," she said.

I examined the lock. If it had been picked it had been a sweet job. "You might want to look around the place and see if anything's missing," I said.

"Oh, God."

"Don't worry. If whoever killed Herbert has been through this desk it isn't you he's after."

"Maybe Herbert just forgot to lock it this time."

"Did he ever forget before?"

"I don't think so."

I went through the letters in the pigeonholes. All bills, addressed to Pingree's office. They didn't tell me anything except that he was a month late paying Detroit Edison and had received a dunning notice from a collection agency employed by the corporation that owned his building. "You'd better look around," I said. "Just this morning someone told me that when something changes in a man's life just about the time he gets dead, it's a change worth checking."

While she was looking I went through the drawers, also unlocked. Stationery, a rack of alphabetical file folders in the deep drawer with nothing in them, a drawer full of receipts, many of them from the speedy-print place across from Pingree's building. Edie returned to my side as I was going through the last. "Nothing seems to be missing."

I closed the drawer. "Did you ever see Herbert put anything in this desk?"

"He had this habit of taking slips of paper out of his wallet and throwing them in that drawer."

"What else?"

"Nothing. Well, a couple of times I saw him take a big manila envelope out of the top drawer and pull something out and look at it, then put it all back."

"You're sure it was a manila envelope?"

"Yes, a big one. Stuffed full. It was starting to split."

I went through the top drawer again, then all the others. I felt inside the compartment under the pigeonholes on top. Just for the hell of it I worked my fingers into the narrow space between the rolltop and the top of the pigeonholes, where things sometimes disappear in desks of that design. I got a splinter under a fingernail from an unfinished edge, nothing more.

"That explains why he didn't toss the apartment," I said. "He got what he was after."

"Do you think that's why Herbert was killed?"

"Either that or he's mopping up. Poor Herb. He was cagey enough to keep his dynamite out of the office and dumb enough to tell his killer where he kept it. Otherwise the guy would've hung around to search the office after Herb died."

"He always thought he was ahead of the pack," she said. "It was cute for a while. God, I can't believe he's dead."

The drawer containing the receipts was still open. Something had rung my doorbell when I first saw them, then run away. Now it rang again. I pointed at the telephone on the end table by the sofa. "Can I use that?"

She said of course. Information gave me the number of the East Detroit printer. I pecked it out. A male voice with a cigarette wheeze answered. I asked it if they did photocopying. The owner of the voice said if it weren't for photocopying they wouldn't have any business at all. I thanked him and hung up.

"What was that about?" Edie asked.

"Maybe Herb wasn't back with the pack all the time." I walked the length of the apartment and back, sucking on my sore finger. I imagined I was a little guy in a loud sportcoat. I stopped in front of a built-in bookcase next to the balcony door. It contained a number of volumes and some Mexican pottery that matched the lamps in the bedroom. "Whose books, yours or his?"

"Most of them are mine. That top row is his. Was his."

Some hardcover detective novels, a couple of trashy best sellers, and a book without a jacket whose green cover caught my eye because I had one just like it in my little home library. *Detroit Is My Own Home Town*, by Malcolm W. Bingay. I slid it out and opened it to the table of contents. I ran my finger down the page, found what I wanted, and turned to that chapter.

Edie was reading past my shoulder. " 'Shall Not Perish From the Earth' ?"

"So they borrowed the heading from Lincoln," I said. "The chapter's about a man named Hazen S. Pingree."

"Herb's great-uncle. Or something."

When I turned the page, a small rectangular brown envelope slid out from between the leaves. I caught it, put the book back on the shelf, and tipped the envelope's contents out into my hand. A small steel key with a short shank and a round tab with a number on it. It belonged to a safety deposit box. I had had three just like it, for as long as it had taken me to possess and get rid of $750,000 in cash. A long time ago. Last week.

"Or something," I agreed.

18

"YOU THINK HERBERT COPIED EVERYTHING THAT WAS IN the big envelope?" Edie asked.

I said, "Those printers' receipts total up to a hefty bill for someone who couldn't pay his utilities. He wasn't just making copies of his hand."

She looked at the watch pinned to her sweater. "I can't go with you to the bank. The assistant principal's teaching my two o'clock, but I have to be back at school for a conference at three."

"Do you have a dollar bill?"

She hesitated, then retrieved her purse from a table near the door and fished a single out of a nest of small bills. I don't know how they do it. Men line theirs up according to denomination, with all the presidents' faces turned the same way, and can't separate one as quickly as a woman can from the wad she carries around. Edie gave me the bill. I pocketed it, scribbled a receipt in my notebook, tore out the sheet, and handed it to her.

"That says you've retained my services to recover property that was stolen from your apartment for a consideration of one dollar. Don't tell anyone about it and put it away in a safe place until I ask you for it. Chances are I never will. Cops get ugly when a citizen messes around in an open homicide case. That paper suggests I'm investigating something else entirely. Call it anti-incarceration insurance.''

"Shouldn't you have a copy?''

I grinned. "If you can't trust a lady schoolteacher. Besides, you don't get your dollar back until you return the receipt.''

"Why are you? Messing around in it, I mean.''

I stopped grinning. "If I knew that I'd know why I'm in this business, and that would only depress me. Let's just say I'm the patron saint of little men in funny clothes who take jobs outside their aptitudes and get killed for it.''

The security buzzer razzed. "Who knows you're home?'' I asked.

"Nobody. I didn't tell them at school where I was going.'' She slid open the balcony door and stepped out, then came back. "A young man in a beige coat. There's a police officer with him.''

"The young one's the Sergeant Trilby I told you about. He's a fast worker is Sergeant Trilby. Is there a back stairs?''

"It leads down to the laundry. The only way out besides the front door is the fire exit. That sets off an alarm.''

"The laundry will do. Give me two minutes and buzz them in.'' I opened the door to the hallway. "It's up to you whether they find out we've been talking, or about the safety deposit box. My job will be smoother if they don't know for a while.''

"I can always tell them I found the key later.''

My grinning muscles had had enough workout for one day. "Two minutes,'' I reminded her.

The buzzer sounded again as I took the hall down the other way to the back stairs. On my way into the basement laundry I passed a bucket-shaped woman in a red-and-yellow muu-muu that made Herbert S. Pingree's sport coat look like an evening with Alistair Cooke. Her hair was a blaze of bobby pins and she was carrying an empty plastic mesh laundry basket. It didn't seem to bother her that I didn't have any washing with me. With neighbors like that, it was no wonder a complete stranger could walk into a security building and search one of the apartments without someone hollering cop.

It was a windowless room with block walls, a bare concrete floor, and a fairly new washing machine and dryer. The washing machine was going. I smoked a cigarette and watched what looked like a rainbow collection of slips and negligees hurtling through the spin cycle with several pairs of white boxer shorts. They looked to be having a lot more fun than I was. After about five minutes I squashed the butt into the floor and left. Nobody yelled freeze as I stepped out the front door.

My office was on the way to the bank. I stopped off to check for mail and government agencies. I had some bills, a letter inviting me as a preferred customer to a preview showing of the winter line at a haberdasher's where I'd bought a scarf for two dollars when I tailed someone there last summer, and William Sahara. This time he was waiting on the upholstered bench in the reception room, reading the *National Geographic* article about dinosaurs. He had on the tan coat over what looked like the same unremarkable gray suit. He probably had a lot of them.

I said, "You didn't like the chair in the office?"

He tossed the magazine onto the coffee table and stood up. "I decided to make this a polite visit. Last night I was ready to kill you."

That clinched it. People who haven't killed say "tear you to pieces" or something equally graphic; plain killing doesn't seem like enough. I hadn't been able to make up my mind whether that counterassassination bit was a stall or not, but now I was sure it wasn't. He knew killing was enough.

"Let's talk," I said, pointing to the office door. "Should I use my key, or do you need the practice?"

"Oh, shut up."

I unlocked the door and held it for him. He kept on the coat and sat down in the customer's chair. He seemed to have overcome his Wild Bill Hickok complex about doors. I hung up my outerwear and took my mail over to the desk and settled into the swivel. He didn't start talking right away, so

111

I took my pen knife out of the drawer, slit open the bills, and read each one before filing it under the blotter. I tossed the haberdasher's letter into the wastebasket and folded my hands on top of the desk and looked at him. The same calm brown eyes behind the amber aviator's glasses, the same brown hair, shorter than regulation but a long way from a military skinhead, the same vague face with the almost-lantern jaw. He was sitting with his legs crossed and his hands resting on his raised thigh.

"You saw Catherine last night," he said.

"Uh-huh."

"We agreed you'd stay away."

"You agreed. I said I didn't want to see her. Doing what we don't want to do is part of being a grown-up."

"What did you talk about?"

I lifted my eyebrows. "You don't know?"

"Damn it, why do you think I wanted to keep you apart? Now a connection has been established between you and me. I told you she was being watched."

"That's an understatement. More people have been watching her lately than saw *Gone With the Wind*."

"What's that mean?"

"How long have you known about Catherine's affair?"

He didn't flick an eyelash. "What affair?"

"I'd be disappointed if you turned out to be just another husband hiring a dick to shadow his wife from motel to motel," I said. "Somehow I don't think I'm going to be disappointed."

"That isn't why I hired you. We've been all through that."

"I wasn't talking about me. I meant Herbert S. Pingree. Trans-Global Investigations. I caught him eavesdropping at the door of a ladies' room with your wife on the other side. Is he the one who told you I was with her?"

"Moss and Wessell told me. They followed you. They're both in the hospital, incidentally. Did you have to use a wrench?"

"They're lucky I wasn't chopping wood. You can't have it both ways, Sahara. Either you paid Pingree to tail Catherine or Moss and Wessell told you about him. He was about as hard to spot as a weather balloon."

He waved it off. "They told me someone else was following her. I knew she was being followed. I'm more concerned that you made contact with her against my instructions."

"Uncle Sam didn't hire Pingree. He isn't *that* hard up." I unfolded my hands. "I don't know the rules of your game, Sahara. To know that, I'd have to know what the game *is*. Okay, say you found out Catherine is having an affair with the man you call Frank Usher. Any P.I. who specializes in divorce work would be happy to take your money to get the goods on them. You didn't have to come here with a story about wanting to quit the Company."

"Walker, Walker." He touched his glasses. "I told you she was being watched and I told you I thought they'd sicced Papa Usher on me. Do you think he wouldn't charm her into bed to get information?"

"I thought about it. It doesn't explain Pingree."

"I didn't know about Pingree until last night when Moss and Wessell called me from your neighborhood. I didn't know his name until you told me just now; last night it seemed more important to talk to you. It's conceivable that Usher sublet his assignment to this Pingree to keep an eye on Catherine when he himself couldn't be with her. That's just a hypothesis. He might have been in a hurry. He might have been misled on the subject of Pingree's qualifications. I'll ask Pingree when I see him. What concerns me—"

"He's dead. Pingree is."

If I was looking for a reaction I wasted some eyesight. He said, "Did you kill him?"

I smiled and shook my head and stripped the cellophane off a fresh pack. "Everybody's copping my lines today. I was going to ask you if *you* killed him."

"That's a fair question. So is mine. After all, he was bothering your ex-wife."

"Women can take care of themselves today. They always could." I unclipped the Smith & Wesson, holster and all,

113

from my belt and laid it on the blotter. "You can check it if you like. There's dust in the barrel."

Sahara didn't move. "Was he shot?"

"Yeah, I really didn't think you'd make a slip that bad. I think it was cyanide poisoning. You ever use it in your work?"

"I don't like it," he said. "It's unpredictable. They pumped enough of it into Rasputin to kill a herd of elk and he was still moving when they threw him in the river. Papa's used it I'm sure. He's been around long enough to have tried everything."

"You didn't answer my question."

"I'm not in the habit of discussing the nuts and bolts of my profession. What do you think was Pingree's part in this?"

"I think he was a stalking horse. Or a stumbling one." I plucked a cigarette out of the pack and played with it, not lighting it. "Somebody hired him to trip over Catherine's footsteps and called a lot of attention to himself to cover whoever was *really* following her. Somebody maybe like you. You said yourself Moss and Wessell were on our heels last night."

"Yours, not hers. So why kill Pingree?"

"He wasn't exactly a clam. He made an appointment to see me at his office this morning. He said he wanted to take me in on whatever he was working. You *sub rosa* types set a lot of store by silence." I didn't mention the theft at Pingree's apartment, or the safety deposit key lying like a tractor weight in my pocket.

"When was he killed?"

I looked at my wristwatch, tapped it, and held it next to my ear to hear the ticking. "Five hours ago, about. I was there just after he fell."

"I was with some people then."

"Did they have names?"

"They will if necessary." He rose. "You know where to reach me if you have any more questions."

"Don't you want a progress report?"

114

"What for? Now that you've been seen with Catherine your cover is blown. All your actions since we first made contact are known or soon will be. Whatever you've done on my behalf is tainted. Now I have to find someone else and start all over again. Did I tell you you're fired?"

"I kind of had that impression."

He grasped the doorknob. "Too bad, Walker. You could've used a friend like me."

"I don't use friends," I said. "Just so you know. I'm investigating Pingree's murder. I have a client."

"You didn't waste any time."

"I hope you'll remember that when someone asks you for a reference."

He shut the door between us. I was still playing with the Winston a minute later, trying to decide whether it was worth setting on fire, when the telephone rang.

"Trans-Desktop Investigations," I said. "Another day, another dollar. Literally."

"You son of a bitch."

"Just a second." I put down the receiver, got up, and poked my head out into the waiting room. Sahara was gone. I went back to the desk and sat down.

"Hello, Catherine. Sounds like old times."

"You know what it's like to have a freckle-faced waitress come into the ladies' room and tell you your gentleman friend's gone home?"

"Not even vaguely. But I'm sorry. Yesterday was a long day." Not as long as today, I thought.

Her tone lost some of its heat. "Well, well. It's learned how to apologize."

"It's had plenty of practice. Was there another reason you called? I have to get to the bank."

"They can wait a little longer for their million," she said. "What happened with the man who's following me?"

"He isn't following you anymore."

"Did he tell you he was working for Bill?"

"It takes a while to tell. Can I call you later?"

115

"No, Bill might come home any time. Will you be at the house tonight?"

"My house?"

"Well, since the settlement. Can I come over tonight? I don't plan to go to bed with you," she added.

"I wasn't planning to invite you. Make it seven."

She said seven would be fine. The connection broke. I cradled the receiver gently, looked at the cigarette, scratched my ear with the filter tip. Then I rolled it into a ball and lobbed it into the wastebasket. Pingree's key and I went to the bank.

19

I DREW THE SAME MACHINE-PUNCHED BLONDE WHO HAD rented me the three boxes when I'd put Gail Hope's three quarters of a million in storage. She keyed me into the vault and left me alone to examine the box's contents in an anonymous little room with a bare table. I sat down and drew out a thick sheaf of coarse copy paper bound with a wide rubber band. The paper smelled of ink and developing chemicals.

Most of the stuff was junk, an eight-month record of failure. Using what looked like college composition books, Pingree had kept scrupulous count of every meager assignment he had managed to scratch up since leaving the River Rouge Police Department; every expense, every setback, every bill he had decided to put off paying in order to satisfy his more impatient creditors. I pictured him sitting in his toy office, filling page after lined page with initials and dates and skimpy dollar amounts in his neat round schoolboy hand while he waited for the telephone to ring or the door to open.

In April he did nothing.

In May he placed an advertisement in the *Free Press* classifieds, painstakingly composing it in one of the books, with many scratchouts and transpositions: "Lost something? Scared? In trouble? Call TRANS-GLOBAL INVESTIGATIONS today for a free consultation. Peace of mind is our stock-in-trade." His office telephone number followed.

117

In June he recorded two attempts on the part of the *Free Press* to collect on the ad. Later that month he landed a security job with a men's store at the Northland Mall. It lasted two weeks, long enough to pay off most of his bills.

In July he didn't work at all.

In August he looked for a woman's lost dog. He didn't find it.

In September he borrowed $250 from Edie to pay his office rent. Two weeks later he borrowed another hundred to keep his telephone from being shut off. At the end of the month he ran a credit check for a St. Louis savings and loan and used the money to repay part of his debt.

The first two weeks of October he twiddled his thumbs and re-read the paperback novels in his desk drawer. Then on the seventeenth he paid Detroit Edison, Michigan Bell, AAA, and his landlord. He repaid the rest of Edie's loan the same day. On the twentieth he wrote a check for $89.50 to Quality Auto Service on Military for repairs to his car heater. The next day he put down a fifty-dollar deposit on a suit at Hudson's pending alterations, and from that point through the first half of November he recorded all bills paid in full. Expenditures for that four-week period came to a little over a thousand dollars.

I looked through the rest of the stuff. Copies of bills and canceled checks, a letter to the woman who owned the lost dog reminding her that she had agreed to pay Pingree his fee regardless of whether he found the dog. No mention anywhere of the source of his sudden income. It seemed a serious lapse for so meticulous a keeper of records.

One item in particular stuck out because it was the only typewritten page in the sheaf, double-spaced on a single sheet with wide margins, a fuzzy copy but legible. It appeared to be made up of times of day and geographical locations. I had just started reading it when the blonde clerk knocked and opened the door to tell me the bank was closing.

I folded the typewritten sheet, put it in my inside breast pocket, snapped the rubber band around the rest, and returned it to the box. She helped me put the box back in the vault. I thanked her and left.

I used a pay telephone downtown to call Edie. "How'd it go with the cops?" I asked her.

"They weren't here long," she said. "I had to tell them you met me at the restaurant. They wanted to know why they couldn't reach me at school and why I wasn't surprised when they told me Herbert was dead. I didn't say anything about your coming back here with me, though."

"You were right not to try and bluff them out." I watched a mounted patrolman threading his big chestnut through the stalled rush-hour traffic on Michigan. The sun had slipped below the clouds, gleaming off his black leather and glowing satiny red on the horse's curried coat; an arrogant, mythic pair, making as much sense against the gray granite backdrop of downtown as a stained-glass window in a cannery. "You didn't mention the key?"

"No. Or the locked desk either. The sergeant asked if Herbert had any enemies or if I knew what he was working on. I said I couldn't help him. I hope I did the right thing."

"So do I."

She didn't pick up on it. "What was in the box?"

"Bills mostly, and all of them paid up. Did he tell you he came into some money recently?"

"No. But then we haven't talked, really talked, for some time. Not since I suggested he move out. It's been a crowded semester for me, and I've been seeing Tim besides."

"Tim?"

"The man I'm—the man I met. Herbert seemed a little preoccupied too. I thought maybe he'd found another security job, or was busy looking for a new place."

"Were you at all curious when he paid off the rest of your loan all in a lump?"

The line was silent briefly. "He recorded the loan?"

"He recorded everything. Up to a point. He had plenty of time. Did you ask him where he got the money?"

"It wasn't important. You have to understand that Herbert wasn't my area of interest anymore. I was happy when he

119

paid me back—not because of the money, but for him. I know how much it hurt him to ask for it in the first place. He might not have looked like it, but Herbert was a proud man. As I said, I assumed he'd found a client and I didn't press him about it.''

"I think it was more than a client," I said. "I think he thought he'd stumbled over the end of the rainbow.''

"What do you mean?"

"If I knew what I meant I'd give you back your dollar. I'll call you when I know." I took the receiver away from my ear.

"Wait! Hello?"

I put it back. "I'm here."

"This working for a dollar; is that normal in the investigating business?"

"It's not a normal business.''

"It makes me more confused than ever about Herbert's reasons for giving up a perfectly good job with the River Rouge Police Department. I grew up in Dearborn. We never quit anything unless something comes along that pays better.''

I leaned against what Michigan Bell calls a booth today. I felt my face showing its age. "Don't look for answers from me," I said. "I'd have to learn a whole new language to explain it, and I don't think the language would have the words I need. Herb would know. He made all the mistakes you can't make when you think along those lines and get out alive, but he'd understand it without my having to go into it. He wasn't born in Dearborn, was he?''

"DelRay, right behind Great Lakes Steel. He said he was ten years old before he discovered sunrises aren't green everywhere.''

"I'll call," I said again, and hung up quickly. Suddenly I couldn't stand talking to her any longer, or anything else female for that matter. As murky as things looked, it was becoming clearer all the time that all Herb had ever wanted was a little attention. He had given up on respect, and when

120

he went for the next best thing he got it from the wrong quarter.

I bought the *News* from a box and read it at a counter down the street over a corned beef sandwich and a cup of coffee while I waited for the traffic to clear. Herb hadn't made the early-evening edition. When I went back out the cars were moving smoothly and there was no sign of the mounted cop or his horse. Well, there was one, and it looked right at home.

The last of the light was glimmering somewhere behind Inkster when I walked into the house and turned on the lights. I turned on all the lights, including the one over the front stoop. I put a lively Dixieland record on the department-store turntable and fixed myself an Edinburgh screwdriver, one part orange juice and three parts Scotch, the sunniest drink I knew. Whistling in the graveyard is getting to be more expensive all the time.

The antique clock in the living room, my only heirloom, had run down. I found the key on the floor behind the book cabinet, wound the mainspring and striker, and twirled the minute hand through five cycles, letting the chimes ring, then set it to the correct time. When the record finished its side I turned it over. As luck would have it, the first cut on the second side was "St. James Infirmary." I thought of Herbert S. Pingree. I would have thought of him anyway.

I got the folded sheet out of the inside breast pocket of my jacket where I'd hung it in the hall closet and spread the sheet out on the table in the kitchen and sat down. Neatly tabulated, the typewritten times of day covered five days, and the corresponding locations all belonged to the city of Detroit and its suburbs. It looked like a record of somebody's movements, and except for the lack of explanatory detail, resembled the notes I kept when I tailed someone. At first it appeared random, as if the subject were a tourist following no itinerary but that dictated by his own curiosity, but a ragged pattern ran through it, like a trickle of water down a pane of glass.

121

At 4:00 P.M. on Tuesday—no date—the subject, whoever he or she was, paid a visit to the Detroit Civic Center. On Thursday at 9:15 A.M., after several other stops at various locations, he was at Joe Louis Arena. At 4:45 P.M. that same day he went to the Renaissance Center. He was back at the Joe on Friday at 6:00 P.M., and at 11:30 P.M. Saturday—the latest he had stayed out—he paid a call on Trappers Alley in Greektown. He had arrived at each place on either the hour or the quarter or the half and had departed after fifteen minutes. The clipped regularity of the visits and their duration suggested a military precision, as of times previously agreed upon between two or more parties. Meetings. Aside from the fact that all of the meetings took place within the downtown area, while his various other ramblings carried him from points as far away as Southfield and Belleville to Grosse Pointe and Flatrock, there appeared to be no connection between the locations chosen.

I circled each of the places with a pencil and sat back to look at them. Something flashed in my tired brain and was gone, like a single dissonant frame inserted in a sixteen-millimeter film. I tried to rewind it for a better look. The wheezy chimes of the old clock in the living room marked seven, wrinkling my concentration. On the end of the last gong the doorbell rang, tearing it to shreds. I put the sheet in a drawer, went into the living room, and peeped between the curtains on the window next to the front door. Catherine had come back to the Walker house after more than ten years.

20

HER EYES WITH THEIR MELANCHOLY TILT TOOK IN THE ROOM behind me, filled with light and loud music, and the glass of orange liquid in my hand. "Somebody must've scared you pretty bad," she said. "I haven't seen an Edinburgh screwdriver since I walked out on you."

I said, "The taste hasn't improved."

She came in past me, trailing something costly with a faintly bitter edge. She was wearing a full-length silver fox coat that covered up whatever she had on underneath, and blue leather boots with killer heels. Her hair looked almost red in the bright light. I closed the door against the beginning of an Arctic winter.

She looked around. "I don't believe it. Nothing's changed."

"I gave away your china pugs," I said. "They reminded me of the carved lions in front of a whorehouse in Saigon."

"Still the genteel conversationalist. Is the hall closet still for coats, or are you hiding brunettes in there now?" She walked out of the fox in one smooth motion, opened the closet door, and flicked through the hangers until she found a wooden one. She wore a schoolmarmish gingham blouse with a ruffle at the throat, tucked into a teal skirt that came down over the tops of her boots. The outfit added a little to her height and accentuated her new athletic trimness.

123

"That's what's different. You used to be a brunette."

"No wonder you're a detective."

"We look at ears, the way a person walks. Things you can't change. Women get a new hair color as often as I clean my gun."

"I see you're not wearing it."

"The night's young."

She leaned in through the open bedroom door, then went into the kitchen. She came back after thirty seconds. "You didn't use to be a good housekeeper. If I were a nosy ex-wife I'd guess there hasn't been a woman in your life for some time."

"There have been too damn many women in my life," I said. "Especially lately. Can I get you a drink, or should I open a vein?"

"I'm not thirsty. Okay if I turn off the music? We never did have the same taste."

"Go ahead." As she turned the knob I excused myself and went into the kitchen. I had every intention of pouring the rest of my drink into the sink, but it didn't get that far. I rinsed out the empty glass and turned it bottomside-up on the drainboard. When I returned to the living room she had switched off all but two lamps and was sitting on the sofa with her legs crossed and her hands folded in her lap, oozing poise out of every pore. I took the easy chair, just oozing. The furnace was now running too well.

"I remember the day we picked out this furniture," she said. "I never thought it would last this long. I was right."

"You picked it out. I threw money at it. Quite a lot of money for what I was making."

"Money never meant anything to you anyway. You were the least ambitious man I'd ever known. From the looks of things you still are."

"How'd you wind up married to a spy?"

"I'm sure Bill's told you all about that."

"That was his side."

"All this liberation talk is for kids. A woman my age can't just go back to college—well, *go* to college, I never exactly

124

got that far the first time—and come out four years older with a degree in botany and expect to compete with all these young bitches born to the Gospel according to Gloria Steinem. My only hope is to attach myself to something promising. I guess I never had the eye for it. I drew a sleuth, a bum, a crook, and a spy, in that order. Bill told me he held a high-level government post. It looked pretty good after what I'd just had.''

"He told me about the gun smuggler."

The corners of her mouth pulled out. "Loose, isn't he? His trade is supposed to be secrecy."

"A trade is a trade," I said. "What makes you think you'll do any better with Edgar?"

"Who's asking, you or Bill?"

"Just curious. Your husband fired me today, by the way. For talking to you."

"No kidding?" She looked pleased for a moment. "I haven't said I'm attaching myself to Edgar. I get attention from him, which is more than I get at home. But if it were to turn into something more serious I could do a lot worse. Let's face it, I'm not going to land a General Motors board member at my age. They're all running around with twenty-year-old blondes."

"Killers don't offer much in the way of security."

"Edgar's no more a killer than you are."

I lit a cigarette and dropped the match into the ashtray on the end table. She watched me. I realized then I was using one of the Dresden saucers she had bought at the old downtown Hudson's. I'd been using it for years without thinking about it. "There's one somewhere in this woodpile," I said. "The name of the little man who was following you was Herbert S. Pingree. I found him this morning in his office, dead. Poisoned."

She unfolded her hands and refolded them the other way. "Did it have anything to do with me?"

"You be the judge." I excused myself again, went back into the kitchen, and came out with the typewritten sheet. I laid it in her lap and sat back down. "Pingree had that under lock and key. It's the kind of record a P.I. keeps when he's tracking someone's movements. Does any of it look familiar?''

She stared at it for several seconds. Then without meeting my gaze she opened her purse, blue leather to match her boots, slid a pair of glasses with rose-colored frames out of a Louis Vuitton case, and put them on. They made her eyes look less sad. She read. ''Why are some of these places circled?''

''Just doodling. Anything?''

''This isn't me.''

''Are you sure?''

''I haven't been to Grosse Pointe in months and I wouldn't be caught dead in Belleville. I've never been to Joe Louis Arena in my life.'' She folded her glasses, returned them to the case, and the case to her purse. She held out the sheet. ''If this is connected with this man Pingree's murder, I don't see where I fit in.''

I accepted the sheet. ''He kept a close record of his employment during the eight months he was in business for himself. It wasn't hard. What there was was penny-ante and his expenses kept on top of him most of the time. Then, starting last month, poof! he had money to burn. Only he neglected to record where it came from. He left something else out as well. He left out you.''

''Then I was right. I don't fit in.''

''You forgot he was following you last night, and probably was the one who'd been tailing you for some time. You weren't anywhere in his records, though. He doesn't mention employment of any kind for the past month. When did you first suspect you were being followed?''

''About a month ago,'' she said. ''I think you ought to talk to Bill.''

''I did, this afternoon. You called the office just after he left. He never heard of Pingree. He says. The world's full of people who never heard of Pingree. I was one of them until last night.'' I peeled the cigarette away from my lip and ground it out in the bottom of the saucer. "How can I get in touch with Frank Usher? You call him Edgar."

"Why?" She was holding her purse in front of her with both hands, an old gesture I remembered.

"I want to ask him some questions. Starting with where he was this morning around nine o'clock."

"He's a gentle old man. He wouldn't hurt a fly."

"I'm interested in Pingrees, not flies." I moved a shoulder. "He doesn't have to talk to me if he doesn't want to. I know a detective sergeant in East Detroit who would be happy to pinch hit. I don't have a client to stand in front of now."

The star-shaped scar on her right cheek disappeared into her sudden pallor. "That would drag me into it. You, too."

"I'm in it," I said. "Lady, I'm in it. Pingree died in my arms."

"You used to protect people. Women especially."

"I thought they needed it then."

"You've really gotten to be a bastard."

"I know. It's the price I paid for becoming a better housekeeper."

She rose icily. "I'll tell Edgar. He'll get in touch with you. You're wasting your time."

"It's not worth much anyway."

I got up and went over and took her coat out of the closet and held it for her. She wrapped it around herself, glanced down at her wristwatch. "It's Friday night. You've just got time to catch the People Mover before it shuts down. Maybe Pingree's mysterious quarry is riding it tonight."

I felt my face grow blank.

She smiled incredulously. The tiny scar was back now. "You didn't notice, did you? I thought when you circled those places—hell, mister, you're some detective."

I took the typewritten sheet out of my pocket and unfolded it. The Civic Center, 4:00 P.M. Tuesday. Joe Louis Arena, 9:15 A.M. Thursday and 6:00 P.M. Friday. The RenCen, 4:45 P.M. Thursday. Trappers Alley, 11:30 P.M. Saturday. The downtown People Mover, Detroit's experiment in mass transit, stopped at all those stations. The entire circuit took fifteen minutes, which was the interval between all the arrivals and departures listed in the report. The dissonant frame I had missed the first time I'd looked at the circled names stood stock still and leered at me.

I refolded the sheet and put it away. Catherine was gone by then. Her laughter hung in the open doorway like the bitter aftereffect of her cologne.

21

I WAS FLOATING SEVERAL STORIES ABOVE THE PAVEMENT. IT was night and I could see the lighted display windows of the shops below on Grand River and Michigan and the pools of pinkish light beneath the street lamps on Woodward and beyond them, wheeling away to the sky, the yellow and orange and blue and green and turquoise lights of a million windows, glittering like insects with hard shiny bodies on fresh tar. I looked away from them, and I wasn't floating at all. I was riding in a train of some kind, balanced on a single high rail that swayed beneath my feet as I stood hanging on to a steel handle to keep from pitching into one of the benches that lined the car on both sides under the windows.

Near me on one of the benches sat a young woman whose honey-blond hair and slightly protruberant blue eyes reminded me of Edie Hibbard's. She was drinking from a large disposable Pepsi cup. I realized suddenly that I was thirsty, desperately thirsty; I had ridges on my tongue like windtracks in loose sand. Edie saw me lusting after the cup, smiled, and offered it to me. I reached out for it. My hand stuck out of a green-and-yellow houndstooth sleeve, and that's how I knew I was Herbert S. Pingree, great-nephew of Hazen (or something), a native of DelRay behind Great Lakes Steel, the president of Trans-Global Investigations: *Lost something? In trouble?* Yes and yes. *Peace of mind is our stock-in-trade.* Rest in peace of mind, dear Herbert. Trade you a stock for one sip from that cup.

Then the cup was in my hand and I was drinking, guzzling, choking, the brown sticky liquid running over my chin. I didn't notice the scorched, bitter smell until the cup was empty. I looked at Edie over the edge of the cup. The protuberant blue eyes were sad now, tilting away sadly from a bold Grecian nose. Catherine's nose, Catherine's eyes. Her sardonic mouth opened to let out a laugh, and as she laughed I smelled her cologne: A scorched, bitter smell. I dropped the cup. It broke like glass when it struck the floor. Then I noticed that Edie-Catherine wasn't alone on the bench. She was seated between an arid-looking man in a gray suit and amber-tinted glasses, and another man, older, ordinary, with a plump face and smoky eyes and dark thinning hair and a neat little moustache, a face from a photograph. They were laughing too. All three of them were having a good time.

I tried to join them, but I couldn't get enough air for a really good guffaw. I could hardly get enough air to breathe; my lungs had gone out on strike. The blood came hot to my face and I knew I was turning purple. They thought that was funnier than anything. They howled. Their mouths opened wider and wider until they formed one great pulsing hole with a black center that looked more inviting than any bar I had ever walked into. My vision was blurring, and for a panicky second I was afraid I'd miss the hole. I didn't. I leaned forward and my toes left the floor of the car and I did a beautiful free fall toward the cool moist black bottom. I knew it would be cool and moist, like dark moss. Their laughter followed me all the way down, colliding and jangling together like so many requiem bells.

The ringing was real. It belonged to the telephone in the living room. My eyelids snapped open like a pair of windowshades, rolling and flapping in an empty skull. I lay there for a moment, hanging on to the mattress with both hands, while the darkness around me separated into familiar shapes in a shaft of skim-milk light zigzagging through the new

130

thermal window in my bedroom, whose double panes turned the three-quarter moon into Siamese twins. When I was sure I was no longer falling, I rolled out from under the covers fully clothed except for shoes and scuffed out toward the source of the ringing. As a nightcap, I decided, an Edinburgh screwdriver is not a glass of warm milk.

The clock read 2:56 when I turned on the light. Whoever wanted me had been ringing a long time. I lifted the receiver and said something in Cro-Magnon into the mouthpiece.

"Mr. Walker?" A deep, heavy voice with a slight trace of cornpone.

"You first," I said.

The owner of the voice chuckled. Some voices are rigged for chuckling. "I guess a little rudeness is the least I deserve for calling so late. Catherine told me you wanted to speak with me."

I felt a little clammy then. Far away the furnace cut in with a thump and a clatter, as if it knew. I lowered myself into the easy chair and squirmed deep into the cushions for warmth. "Do I have to call you Papa?"

"At the moment I'd prefer Edgar, or Mr. Pym if you're the formal kind."

"Not Frank Usher, huh."

"A name is just clothing. Where and when would you like to meet? I prefer someplace open. I spent most of my time out-of-doors as a boy, and I guess you could say I'm in my second childhood. This time through I aim to enjoy it."

I thought. Part of me was still suspended in the black hole. "I'll meet you in front of Ford Auditorium. Nine in the morning okay?"

"Two in the afternoon would be better. I'm up way past my bedtime now."

"I'm looking for answers," I said. "I hope you're planning on bringing plenty."

"I'll bring some. How many I go home with is up to you. The older I get, the more I want to know. Life's just a backwards mule, ain't it?"

The accent came down heavily on the last part. I said two o'clock would be satisfactory.

"Good. Nice dreams, son." The connection went away.

22

FOUR HOURS LATER I SHOWERED HARD, SHAVED, AND DRANK
a pot of black coffee strong enough to float the deficit. To
avoid picking up the nightmare where I'd left off I hadn't
gone to bed right away after Usher's call, but had smoked a
couple of cigarettes and watched the last half-hour of *Night
of the Living Dead* on Channel 7. I thought it was a documentary.

Pingree made the front page of the morning *Free Press*
under the headline POISON SUSPECTED IN EAST DETROIT
DEATH. It was a four-inch-square item printed below the fold
with no picture or mention of the dead man's occupation.
The body was reported to have been discovered by an associate. Sergeant Eugene Trilby of the East Detroit Police Department's Criminal Investigation Division was quoted as
saying that he didn't suspect product tampering was involved. The autopsy report was still pending.

I got into a white shirt, gray suit, and black knitted tie and
collected my hat and coat on my way out the door. I never
put them on; the temperature had pulled one of those Michigan late-autumn dipsy-doodles and shot up into the high
fifties. At the office I separated the bills from the junk, ran a
skip-trace for an agency in San Francisco on a disabled city
bus driver who had ducked out on a charge of flagrant misuse
of food stamps, and found him an hour later perched happily

on the local welfare roll, all without leaving my desk. Nero Wolfe, Mycroft Holmes, and the Old Man in the Corner had nothing on me. Dale Leopold used to say that you could tell the real pros by their hemorrhoids.

After calling in the information to San Francisco I typed up a bill and sealed it in a neat envelope complete with a window and *A. Walker Investigations* printed in tasteful blue in the upper left-hand corner. It was one of a thousand I had accepted in lieu of my fee from a printer whose runaway senile father I had found working at McDonald's. While I was returning the old Underwood to its resting place atop the file cabinet, the sixteen-millimeter projector that was my brain stuttered on yet another frame that had no business being on that reel. This time I wound it back and isolated the frame. I grinned. If the day continued as it had started out, I would consider giving up sleep entirely.

At noon I rewarded myself with a full sit-down lunch at a seafood place on East Grand River on the way to Ford Auditorium. I had abalone out of season, baked in a mild horse-radish sauce, and poured a glass of Liebfraumilch in after it to let it swim. My system, bulked up on burgers and fast-food chicken, attacked it like feral dogs. The business has its days. It's the years you want to watch out for.

Appropriately enough in view of its two namesakes, the Henry and Edsel Ford Auditorium in the riverfront Civic Center looks a little like an air filter. At night the mica-flecked blue granite of its curved front wall shimmers like an anaconda's back in the floodlights, but by daylight it looks like plain steel mesh. I stood on the concrete park in front among a shuffling crowd of Saturday celebrants enjoying the unseasonal sun and looked for a man of about sixty who might have resembled the subject of the photograph in my pocket when it was taken thirty years ago. I wasn't looking too hard. I was thirty minutes early for our appointment.

"Mr. Walker?"

He was standing in the shadow of the porch that ran across the front of the building, a stoutish man with a late-middle-age belly swelling below his belt, wearing a coat of some kind of inexpensive tweed and green double-knit slacks and a wide white belt with patent-leather shoes to match. For his age, he was dressed as inconspicuously as William Sahara in his unremarkable grays; you know you're getting on when you wake up one morning with an uncontrollable urge to dress like the Loch Ness Pimp. The fat red eye of a cigar glowed in the dimness of the porch.

"Usher," I said.

"Pym. Step in out of the sun. It's bad for you, you know."

I joined him under the roof. The shade touched the back of my neck, chilling me to the balls of my feet and reminding me that Christmas was only five weeks off, together with the Canada clippers that blast down the river and leave the city dead white in their wake. Up close, his face was less full than in the picture: His cheeks swayed like empty sails when he moved his head and his skin had an orange tint of advancing jaundice. His eyes were still smoky, with the milky beginnings of a cataract in the right, and although his widow's peak had thinned and receded, his moustache had grown fuller and healthier and white as bone. The thick brown smell of his cigar brought memories of Sundays when my uncle came to visit. An uncle I never had. It was that kind of a smell. He was leaning slightly on a blackthorne stick with a brass ferrule and a curved natural grip like a shillelagh.

"You're younger than I expected," he said. "But then everyone's younger than he ought to be these days. I guess that's something an old fogy would say."

I said, "You're not that old and I'm not that young. I didn't come here to play Andy Hardy to your Judge."

"Easy, son."

"I'm not your son, either."

He smiled behind the moustache. "Now, who can say that with any certainty? Where would you like to go?"

"Let's walk. Something tells me this porch is worse for me than the sun."

He pulled on the cigar, blew a wreath, and walked out of the shadows. I hung back a second, watching the way he

135

moved. I couldn't tell if he was carrying. You can't with the professionals. I caught up with him.

We started along the river. The water was pewter-colored and steamed a little in the warmer air. On the Windsor side the skyline had been cut with a scalpel out of gray cardboard, a reflection in a time-delayed mirror of an earlier, cleaner, less belligerent Detroit. Canada was behind us in many ways, but she'd get in step. .

Usher walked with his white head down, holding the cigar down at his side between his fingers like a cigarette when he wasn't pulling at it. When he was, the fiery tip burned back a quarter-inch at a time and trailed smoke like a dirty banner. "I decided to have a talk with you before you got hurt," he said. "More civilians get mashed up in these things than you can imagine. Certainly more than you hear about."

"What's Catherine, a draftee?"

"I'd rather leave her out of this discussion. I hope I can depend on your confidence where she's concerned."

"Not if I think she might get mashed up along with all the other unreported statistics."

He nodded, swinging the stick a little as he walked. "I guess that's fair enough. She don't like you much. Guess you know that."

"It's mutual. But there's a difference between not liking someone and standing by with your hands in your pockets while she walks under a falling piano."

"I like that. Yes I do. Where I grew up we tried to keep our women out of harm. That's old hat now. I'm glad I ain't the only one who's too stiff to change."

I was beginning to see his pattern. When the talk became personal, out came the grits and rustic grammar. I wondered if it was a pattern he'd gotten up for my benefit. I'd been around older people enough to know better than to trust them; and if what Sahara had told me was true, this one had been outwitting European black marketeers, not the world's most gullible lot, years before I was born.

"What's your interest in William Sahara?" I asked.

"What did he say it was?" He waved the cigar. "Oh, I

know you met down in the concourse and again at your office. Just because he shook one tail don't mean I didn't have others.''

"All drawing federal wages, I suppose. He said he wanted out of the Company. You know that much already or you wouldn't have been tailing him in the first place. He wanted me to make the arrangements. Maybe you know that too.''

"I guessed. He say anything else?''

"Only that he wanted to go alone. Catherine wasn't to know anything about it. The town's full of people walking around on tiptoe trying to keep Catherine from knowing anything about anything. Your turn.''

"People quit the Company every day,'' he said. "Agents with a lot more secrets to tell than Sahara. Threat of federal prosecution is usually enough to keep them quiet, but sometimes a book contract or the talk-show circuit is too tall a temptation and then we have to swallow the cod-liver oil and make a statement that don't mean nothing and then we go on same as always, maybe minus some deadwood for the wolves, but that's the game. If we went around slaughtering every field man who hands in his ticket, we'd be a lot shorter on applicants than we already are. We ain't kill-drunk zombies, no matter what they write about us in the Washington *Post*.''
He struck the wooden decking sharply with his stick. "Sahara stole something from Company files. Washington wants it back.''

"And Sahara's head in a dispatch case.''

"My discretion. My instructions are not to negotiate.''

"Some discretion.''

He smiled at the decking. "Contrary to what the polls say, the gents in power do learn from their past fumbles. If no one actually gives the order, no one has to stand the blame in front of a Congressional subcommittee on something-or-other. See, they don't mind being a party to murder, but they're shy about committing perjury.''

"Sahara calls it counterassassination.''

"Bullshit. He's a butcher like the rest of us.''

We separated to avoid breaking up a strolling couple. The ⸱

137

boy was carrying books and the girl had on a Wayne State University sweatshirt.

"What'd he take?" I asked.

"An extensive list of deep-cover agents stationed across the country, together with their locations and the names they're operating under. Nobody's supposed to have access to that file but the director and one or two of his top aides. Sahara got the code somehow. Washington thinks he's planning on selling the list to the enemy. They ain't seen fit to tell me just who the enemy is, but I'm sure it's some subversive element just waiting for its chance to kick Uncle Sam in the nuts and piss on the flag."

"So that's what Washington thinks."

"*I* think it's more than likely he plans to sell the list back to the Company. Oh, he's getting out, all right, but the standard pension ain't good enough. It ain't, by the way; which is why I'm still here in the traces while most of the boys I started out with are back home scraping aphid shit off their roses."

"So how come Sahara's still walking around? The way I hear it, you're death in large doses."

"My job's to get back the list, don't forget. Since he ain't asshole enough to carry it around with him, I need to get a handle on all the places he visits so I can start narrowing down hiding places. I figure he's got to take it out and look at it from time to time, the way a miser counts his coins. I been through all his effects."

"I thought only the dead had effects."

He smiled again. "Well, you caught me with my pants down that time, son. I'm getting ahead of myself."

"Then Catherine's an effect."

"Cat's a special lady, but I guess you know that. If she wasn't I'd have stopped seeing her soon as I found out she knows less about her husband than a grasshopper. Like I said, we ain't zombies. Not all of us."

"Herbert S. Pingree," I said.

"Ah."

138

"If you'd said, 'Herbert who?' I'd have pushed you in the river."

He blew a chain of smoke rings. They drifted toward Windsor, each one widening until it broke noiselessly, like ancient promises. "Don't let this here snowy roof lead you into trouble, son. I don't push as easy as I look."

"Pingree," I repeated.

"I knew about him. Hard not to. I thought I knew some *politicians* who were in the wrong racket."

"Did you hire him to follow Catherine?"

"Now, why would I do that? I was with her most of the time myself."

"Maybe you were paying him to keep an eye on her the rest of the time."

"Son, if I had to I could get people who could follow you into the shower and you'd never know they were sharing your soap. Mostly I work alone, and when I don't, I don't go into the private sector. Even if I did, that boy wouldn't make the top one hundred names on my list."

"Who hired him if not you?"

"If I was to guess, I'd say maybe ol' Sahara thinks more about the little woman than he lets on. Maybe he paid Pingree to see what other roosters was hanging around the henhouse while he was away. Especially this here rooster."

"No good. He had better people for that. They were in the Club Canaveral the night I braced Pingree in the toilet."

"Following you, I expect."

We were running out of deck. One of the last of the season's ore carriers was gliding up the river on the Canadian side, its stacks lisping brackish smoke. We stopped to watch it. I took the typewritten sheet out of my inside breast pocket and handed it to him. He squinted at it. Watching him and Catherine trying to read a menu must have been worth the price of the meal. "Cat told me about this," he said. "You say you got it from Pingree?"

"From his effects." I tried not to stress the last word.

"Rendezvous." He folded it and gave it back. "Why else would someone ride the People Mover around its whole circuit, unless he's a tourist? He gets on at one station, whoever he's meeting gets on at the next. After they finish talking each man gets off where he got on. I'd say your boy Pingree was using both sides of the ruler. Following Cat *and* Sahara.''

''What makes it Sahara he was following?''

''Auction.'' He drew one last time on the cigar and tossed it into the water. It spat once and bobbed on the ore carrier's corrugated wake. ''Sahara's got other buyers for the list of agents. He meets them in a nice public place like the People Mover to discuss terms. Only he got so greedy about it he didn't notice Pingree shadowing him. Not the kind of mistake a man like Sahara usually makes, but you'd be surprised how many steps you miss when the stake's personal.''

I put the sheet away. ''Pingree didn't type this. He didn't have a typewriter in his office or his apartment. He kept his records in script. I didn't give it much thought until today while I was putting away my own machine. So I guess there's something in what you say about missing steps.''

''How you figure he got hold of it if he didn't make it himself?''

A chain clanked on the carrier's steel deck, sounding as loud across the half-mile of water as if it had been dropped at our feet.

''I figure you gave it to him,'' I said, very low. ''Not long before you killed him.''

23

PAPA FRANK USHER WAS STILL WATCHING THE IRON BOAT, his balding, moustached profile looking as if it had been struck out of yellow alloy. "Not too pretty, is she?" he said. "A dignified lady, though, call her that. When I was six I wanted to be a riverboat pilot more than anything. By the time I was ten, the last of the old paddlers had gone to firewood and floating restaurants. Sometimes I think if it wasn't for that I wouldn't be doing what I'm doing. Or maybe I would. I was brought up Calvinist, and I still think all the molds were poured long ago."

I said, "I wanted to be a cowboy, but the first horse I climbed on thought I was a fly. I fell off and you missed the boat and Pingree's dead and here we are. Why cyanide?"

"Cyanide." He was still looking at the carrier. "You'd think they'd have developed something better by now. I took cyanide in Vienna. I was in with this bunch of retired storm troopers and somebody in my own office tipped them. They had me cold in this basement room with no windows. My instructions in a case like that were pretty specific, so I bit down on this capsule I'd been carrying around for six months. The glass cut my lip and I winced and most of it went down my chin. When I went into convulsions a young fellow named Strendle gave me mouth-to-mouth until I started breathing again on my own. I wasn't in no condition to talk after that, so the others left me alone with Strendle. By then I guess he figured he'd bought some stake in my continued well-being, because he helped me escape that night. Sicker than a dog I was, but I kept on walking till the MPs found me. That boy saved my life twice that night. They killed him later."

"The Nazis?"

"No, the Allies. Seems Strendle was personally responsible for the massacre of sixty-seven Jews at Birkenau. They found him guilty at Nuremberg and hanged him." He turned my way. "No, son, I wouldn't feed nobody cyanide. Next time someone tells you it's a humane way to die, you tell him to go ahead and hold his breath until he faints. That'll give him some idea of what it's like. I'm a killer, not a sadist."

"I didn't think you killed him personally. I was just asking for a professional opinion. I think you followed Sahara long enough to put together this itinerary, then switched your attention to Catherine so she'd feel guilty when she found out she was being shadowed by a private detective. You hired Pingree for that, knowing he'd blow it and call attention to himself and cause a confrontation between her and Sahara. She'd be that kind. Only she came to me instead.

"You weren't finished, though. You fed the itinerary to Pingree and turned him loose on Sahara. I don't know what you told him, but I'll bet you flashed your credentials and read him the national security speech. He ate it up, along with a nice retainer, and agreed to keep his mouth shut, even in his business records. Sahara would tumble to him quicker than Catherine. Maybe he'd panic and take off with the list and you'd nail him with it on his person. First, though, he'd flick Pingree away like a mosquito. It was the same as if you'd killed him yourself, Usher. He wasn't much, just a little guy in the wrong racket. I don't know the rules of your game, but it seems to me these little pieces you blow down when you twirl the spinner are supposed to be the object."

He raised his stick and studied the ferrule. I stepped back a pace, but he just flicked at it with his thumb and returned it to the ground. "If someone was to do that, it'd be a bad thing," he said finally. "But if the names on that list got into the wrong hands, there'd be funerals clear across the country."

"That song never plays. Not unless you sang it for Pingree first."

"We do what we do, son. Why we do it ain't always so clear. Nothing is, without uniforms. Maybe nothing ever was."

"Is that a confession?"

He turned away from the carrier and started back along the river the way we'd come. I fell in beside him. A bank of soiled clouds had moved in front of the sun and the air coming off the water was dank, like a gust off an old barrel. He said, "If I wanted to flush Sahara out, why didn't I just make an anonymous call, tell him somebody was on to him?"

"He wouldn't have fallen for it. He and you have been playing the double-reverse so long you wouldn't know a direct approach if it rolled over you. Maybe Pingree's partly responsible. Maybe he tried to sell Sahara that itinerary the way Sahara was peddling the list of agents. I doubt it, though, or the last thing he'd have wanted was a partner to split the take. The only time we met he offered to kick half the job over to me, a complete stranger. Maybe you told him to pose as a blackmailer. Maybe he had just enough smarts to suspect something was wrong with the whole business, and that's why he made me that offer, to get my opinion. Either way you killed him. You might as well have gone up there and handed him that glass of water yourself."

"It won't stick, son, even without the maybes. You need chain of evidence."

"Lawyers need evidence. I fly by my gut. Anyway, you've got some kind of license to kill, so why not humor me and confess?"

"If I did have one, it would only be valid as long as I kept my own mouth shut."

"You haven't denied it."

"All right, it didn't happen."

"Killers lie just like everyone else."

"Not this one," he said. "Not unless he has to. I'm prob-

143

ably the only good ol' boy from my home county that don't get a boot out of it."

I blew some air. "I didn't care for the story much myself. It took too many left turns for my taste. That's why I thought the government had to be involved."

"Well, I wish you luck with it, son. Just don't get between me and Sahara. There's no percentage in it for a citizen."

"I wish to hell you civilized sons of bitches would make a threat when you make a threat. Every one of you borrows his dialogue from Graham Greene."

"I wouldn't know how to begin to make one. You got any rattlers up here?"

The change of subjects threw me for a second.

"Rattlesnakes? Some massasauga. They might bite you if you step on them hard enough."

"I was thinking of the western diamondback. Pound for pound they're the deadliest thing on this continent, but not one of them's a match for your common barnyard hog. You want to know why?"

"Does it matter?"

"They rattle before they strike. Can't help it, it's in their nature. That hog, as soon as he hears that sound he goes after it with his hooves and teeth. Don't take but a few seconds. I ain't heard tell yet of a hog ever losing that fight."

"So the moral is, strike before you rattle."

"That ain't it."

"What is?"

"Stay away from hogs."

We parted where we'd met, in front of Ford Auditorium. He changed hands on the stick and held out his right. "It's been a pleasure, son. I been in the woods so long I forgot what a man looks like."

"Leave Catherine alone."

He shrugged and returned his hand unshaken to the stick. "I was going to tell her good-bye tonight anyway. Maybe you'll say it for me. Tell her I died or I went back home or I got arrested for messing around with eleven-year-old girls.

144

You can make up a lie just as good as I can. That's a compliment. I made up some of the best."

"You are a lie. You and your whole tribe."

"That's a fact. But like all lies we got to play out our string. Good luck again, son. Mind what I said about the hogs."

I said nothing. He stepped onto the porch and went around the curve of the mica wall. I heard his stick tapping for a while.

The cold was thickening and there was a brassy smell of snow in the air. I took my coat and hat off the back seat and put them on before driving back to the office. There I shut myself in; a redundancy in that building, empty of a Saturday. As empty as my head. I sat behind the desk and swiveled my chair toward the window and looked at the roof of the building next door and listened to the foundation crumble under me. I thought about pouring myself a drink. I thought about it some more. Thinking about it was almost as good as drinking it, and a lot easier on the liver. I wondered if I was on to something. I could write a book: *The Cosmic Cockeye*. I might sell a million before the government figured out a way to tax metaphysical boozing.

"I guess if you have to work weekends that's the way to do it."

I swiveled to face Sergeant Trilby. I hadn't switched on the buzzer that tells me someone has entered the outer office and he'd let himself through two doors with none of the club-footed telegraphy of the previous generation of peace officers. He had on a tan corduroy sport coat with chamois patches on the elbows over a V-neck sweater and a pink shirt with a maroon tie. Blue jeans and topsiders. All showing rough use, the uniform of the perennial undergrad, if the college had more green growing up its walls than on its grounds. He was carrying a briefcase under one arm, the soft vinyl kind without a handle.

"I thought the brass was favoring vests this year," I said.

"In East Detroit we're a little more casual. Especially on

145

Saturday. When no one answered the phone at your house I thought I'd see if I could find you here. I'm on my way to Detroit Police Headquarters with some evidence for their lab and it wasn't that much of a detour.''

"Nice of you to think of me. I'd offer you a drink, but I have to see your driver's license first.''

"Never touch it. So this is where you get to work when you went to detective class.''

"I apologized for that crack.'' I pointed my chin at the briefcase. "That the evidence? Nice case. Goes with your outfit.''

He laid it on his side of the desk without answering and sat down in the customer's chair. He propped his right ankle on his left knee and grasped the ankle with both hands. "We got the cutter's report on Pingree. Came in two hours ago.''

I lifted my brows politely.

"Hydrocyanic acid,'' he said. "Thirty grains, give or take. Enough to kill a basketball team full of Pingrees and the mascot. You'd be surprised how easy cyanide is to lay hands on; I was, when I asked the toxicologist. Peach leaves, peach pits, apple seeds—cripes, it's the poison in mercury poisoning, and you can get *that* from fish. So much for canvassing all the local pharmacists, although we're doing that anyway. Any ninth-grade chemistry student can distill himself a batch in his basement with enough kick to wipe out the faculty. And we were worried about crack.''

"It's a dangerous old world, Sergeant. But you knew that.'' I wondered where this was going.

"You frisked Pingree's office, didn't you?''

I scratched my ear. I wanted a smoke, but I didn't want him to think I was stalling. Finally I figured the hell with it and broke one out and got it burning. "I frisked it. It seemed like the thing to do. I thought I was more careful than that. Or are you just fishing?''

"We lifted a partial thumb from his appointment book. Prints don't wipe so well off paper. When it didn't match Pingree's I played a hunch and Faxed it to Lansing. The state police have a full set of yours on file, as they do all private

146

investigators they license in the State of Michigan. What'd you find?''

"Just a lunch date he'd made with Edith Hibbard, his roommate. She told you I kept it for him.''

"Did she?''

"Come on, Sergeant. I know the order of the universe. If she didn't tell you, you got it from the staff at the Black Bull. I hope they were kind to me in their descriptions.''

"She told us. And we got the lunch date off the next sheet on the pad, the old edge-of-the-pencil trick like you read in Agatha Christie. It works about as often as that line about not leaving town. You didn't find anything else?''

I used the ashtray. "If I did, I'd be pretty stupid to admit it now, having withheld evidence in a murder for more than twenty-four hours. By now you've checked me out with Thirteen Hundred downtown. Some of them have told you I'm square as the Old North Church and some of them have told you I'd lie about the time of day in a clock shop. All of them are right, so far as they go.''

"I want to hear it anyway.''

"I didn't find anything but a little dust, and not much of that. The amount of business Pingree did in that office wouldn't have distracted him from his housekeeping.''

He took a hand off his ankle and held his thumb and forefinger an eighth of an inch apart. "I came that close to sending a unit for you when the word came back from Lansing on that partial. Warrant, handcuffs, the works. Then I reminded myself I'm one of the New Breed. You know, Freud in one pocket, Blackstone in the other. We don't clip our toenails in public or beat suspects to death in the squad room. Not on Saturdays. The part of me that was trained by the sort of cop who practices twirling his nightstick in front of a mirror wanted to get you into interrogation without your belt and shoelaces. The part of me that signed up for a night course in Abnormal Psychology wanted even more to come down here and ask you why you're so interested in the murder of someone you say you only knew for fifteen minutes.''

I said, "I'm a curious man, Sergeant. It's one of the reasons I sit here day after day on my college degree and take jobs a cat wouldn't bury for no money to speak of. I get to study the human condition, and I don't even have to sign up for a night course. The number of clients you didn't trip over on your way in here tells you I've got some time on my hands just now. When a harmless little guy like Pingree gets himself killed in a flashy way, I don't want to wait to read about it in the papers.'' I looked at my watch. "If you're going to feed me the lay-off-or-else speech I wish you'd get to it and go. Nine hours is as long as I'm willing to work on weekends.''

"You're a liar.''

"That's the Old Breed talking.''

"I think you two were working something,'' he said. "It wouldn't be the first time we caught a bereaved partner rifling the office for cash or dope or whatever. I think you know who killed him and why, and if you don't know you've got a good idea. As long as we're checking watches, you have forty-one hours left to come to us with the package. After that it won't matter which breed I belong to, I'll send the wagon and you can cool your curiosity at County until I'm good and ready to hear what you have to say.''

"You'll need a charge.''

"We talked to the neighbors. The cleaning crew was in early yesterday, there was an old lady sweeping up and a window washer on the fifth floor. The executive in charge of real property for the corporation that owns the building is in the Cayman Islands with his secretary, probably surfing on his bank account, so we don't know yet what company the crew works for. The only other visitor to Pingree's floor seems to have been the owner of a man's voice his closest neighbor heard through the wall. It could have been your voice. I don't know how they do things down here, but in East Detroit, suspicion of murder sticks long enough to sort some things out.''

I leaked smoke. "Oh, that. I've been in County a couple of times. It's my Cayman Islands. It wouldn't change the fact that I don't know who killed Pingree. You don't think I did it or you'd have come in here with help and called the newspapers later."

He put his foot on the floor, leaned forward, and unzipped the briefcase. "Pingree shared a toilet down the hall with the other offices on the floor. There's a crawl space behind the radiator with a panel that comes off so the plumber doesn't have to punch holes in the wall to get to the pipes. The screws were rusty, but there was fresh steel showing in the slots where someone had been at work recently with a screwdriver. Otherwise we never would have thought to look behind the panel."

I watched him remove a thick manila envelope and put it on the desk in front of me. It was stuffed full, splitting at the seams. The pre-printed address label; from the Professional Investigators Book Service of Denver, Colorado, was made out to Herbert S. Pingree. I thought I knew what was inside, and it threw every theory I had straight into the dumper.

24

THE THICK SHEAF OF PAPERS WAS STICKING OUT THROUGH the wrinkled flap. I put out my cigarette, pinched the bottom of the envelope, and pulled it free of its contents. I went through the stuff slowly, as if I were reading it for the first time. The composition books made me think of school. *How I Spent My Summer Vacation*, by Herbert Selwyn Pingree. Camping, swimming, drinking hydrocyanic acid. *Lost something?* Only my best lead. *In trouble?* Just with the law. *Call A. WALKER INVESTIGATIONS today for a free consultation. A kick in the head is our stock-in-trade.* I felt Trilby's eyes on me like twin augers. And I had thought they weren't cop's eyes.

I was looking for something, but when I found it I didn't spend any more time with it than I had with the other stuff. The page had been typed on heavy stock with a ribbon that needed replacing, hence the fuzzy copy I had been rapping my head against since yesterday. I went on through the bills and other miscellany to the end. It didn't take me as long as it had the first time, but I didn't just thumb through it either. Trilby watched me the whole time. When I was done I put everything back in order, straightened the edges, poked it back into the envelope, and sat back.

"Any of it spell anything?" asked the sergeant,

"I wish I had his hand. I have to type up all my notes or I can't read them the next day."

"The penmanship is satisfactory and the grammar is well above average, not a dangling participle or a misplaced first predicate in a carload. His arithmetic is okay too. I don't know where he stood in geography, because I never got the chance to ask him the state capitals. When I want a handwriting analysis I'll ask my sister. She does horoscopes too. She told me to avoid the company of jackass private eyes today, but I didn't listen. You know what I want."

"Just an observation. He might as well have used Sanskrit for what I got out of it. He kept an adequate record of a crummy practice, that's it."

"What about that typewritten piece? Everything else is in longhand."

"A list of things to do, maybe, places to go. Maybe he bought a machine, didn't like it, and took it back. I know a P.I. who used a shotgun on a brand-new word processor the first time it stuttered and lost an entire surveillance report."

"Funny you should mention a surveillance report," he said.

I cocked a hand. "It could be that. A damn sketchy one. Standard procedure is to record the subject's actions at the places he visits and who he meets. Take pictures if possible. I didn't see a camera in Pingree's office."

"His girlfriend said he talked about buying one and kept putting it off because he didn't know an F-stop from the FAA. Notice anything else about this stuff?"

"Only that he was flush toward the end, settling bills and things. Maybe he hit the daily double at Hazel Park."

"The horses don't run in November. If he had a client, why wasn't it in his records?"

"Maybe for the same reason he went to so much trouble to hide them. Ask your sister. Astrology isn't my racket."

"I'm wondering what is."

"Look around, Sergeant," I said. "This is it, this and a secondhand car and a little place outside Hamtramck you could blow over with garlic on your breath. It's a successful business as far as it goes, but I'd trade it for a corner bar in Sterling Heights in a hot minute. You listen to the same problems in that line of work, but you don't have to offer solutions. If I'm working all the angles, I'm worse at it than Pingree was."

"Not quite. You're still alive." After a moment he stood, returned the package to the briefcase, and zipped it shut.

"Did I pass?"

He looked at me. I nodded toward the case. "That face-reading dodge is as old as bullets."

"It isn't a pass-fail proposition. B-plus."

"Not A?"

"No one rates an A." He glanced at his watch. "Forty hours and eleven minutes."

"You're fast. I've got five-forty-four."

"That's a switch. We're usually a little behind in the suburbs. We like it that way."

I sat there for a while after he left. My brains were in the same condition as the ground-out butt in the ashtray. Pingree hadn't been killed for his papers, or if he had, the killer hadn't found them. But if that were the case, the killer would have torn his apartment inside-out when they didn't turn up in the locked desk, the hiding place Pingree had betrayed somehow in his trusting way. If he had betrayed it. If not, the killer would have tossed the office as the most likely place instead of ducking out while Pingree was still reeling from the effects of the poison. None of that worked. What worked was that no one had jimmied the lock on the rolltop desk; it hadn't been locked in the first place, because Pingree's papers were safely hidden in the wall of the toilet down the hall from his office. An empty gesture; the killer had never bothered to search for the papers. So why was Pingree dead? When my head started to throb I closed up and went to dinner. I don't know where I went or what I ate when I got there. I was chewing on an entirely different plane.

I gave up finally and bought the evening *News* from a stand and went through it on the sidewalk under a street lamp, with my breath curling in front of the print. An item on Page Two confirmed that cyanide had figured in yesterday's death of an East Detroit man and went on to rehash everything I'd read in the *Free Press* that morning. I wasn't interested in the news anyway. I checked the movie listings, but I'd seen all the movies playing around town that didn't have Roman numerals in their titles. The television lineup had the usual Democratic Party rallies with laugh tracks and a documentary program about murderers on the loose.

Around the corner from my house I went into a video place and rented a VCR and two movies. One was *High Sierra*, which had some lines I hadn't memorized yet. The other, a serendipitous discovery in the Action and Adventure section, was *V-8 Vampires*, starring Gail Hope.

At home I spent twenty minutes with the instructions for installation and five minutes doing the installing after throwing away the instructions. I fixed myself a drink—without orange juice this time—poked *V-8 Vampires* into the slot, and switched off the lamp to watch the movie in darkness.

It was a period piece all the way, shot in Southern California on a joke budget with an electric-guitar score, lots of yellow sand and creaming surf, and endless scenes of dotted lines darting under the wheels of black Mustangs and Red Chevy 409s with flames painted on their fenders. The plot was a mishmash about a gang of teenage hot-rodders who divided their nights between drag races downtown and sucking the blood of exclusively blonde bikini beauties on the same desolate stretch of moonlit beach, led by a 500-year-old sexpot with an addiction for plasma and leaded gasoline. Gail Hope played the vampire honcho, and she was almost the only member of the cast who delivered her lines as if they had just occurred to her and weren't pasted on someone's forehead. The climax, in which the Malibu dawn caught her miles from the safety of her coffin in the cellar of an abandoned disco, was genuinely bone-freezing, especially when she began to show her true age and looked like hell served for dessert in her halter top and leather hip-huggers. It was one of her most popular pictures, and one of her last. Her light began to fade soon after, partly because of the bad

153

publicity connected with her affair with gangster Sam Lucy and partly because, by the early 1970s, nothing seemed so quaint or so far removed from reality as the decade of Andy Warhol, beach orgies, and the Age of Aquarius. It was a tough break for someone blessed with the talent to rise above a turkey like *V-8 Vampires*.

I finished my drink in a happy glow. The combination of old movies and alcohol instills a calm in me that other people find in pharmaceuticals. I didn't play *High Sierra*. While the first tape was still rewinding, I put on the lights, got a card out of my wallet on the dresser in the bedroom, and dialed the number I found there. I felt like a projectionist threading the last reel through the gate.

25

AN ALLEY OF LIGHT IN A DARKENED CITY, GREEKTOWN approaching midnight Saturday was crowded with a kind of desperate festivity, like the last corner on earth still untouched by a drifting cloud of radiation. The restaurants were all brightly lit and wild string music stumbled out of doorways where during the day old men in soft caps and loose clothing sucked on bottles of ouzo before going home to Madison Heights and Harper Woods. Trappers Alley, where you went when you were authentically Greeked out, bustled with weekenders riding the arcade escalators and browsing in the knickknack shops and eating Chinese. It was all very foreign to someone who remembered a community the size of a small city where half-naked men wrestled behind the Lafayette Bar and dumpy women who spoke little English wrung the necks of geese in their tiny backyards. A long memory is not a comfort in the City of Detroit.

In Trappers Alley I took two escalators to the top level and bought a People Mover token at a newsstand from a cashier who looked as Greek as Muhammad Ali. I had on wool pants, sneakers, and a zippered jacket with a down lining over a flannel shirt. The outfit wasn't warm enough for the weather—a shardlike mixture of snow and freezing rain was crackling outside on the sidewalk—but I needed to be able to move around and to get to the Smith & Wesson riding in the hollow of my back without having to use a metal detector.

A bored transit cop wearing a leather Windbreaker and a shiny Colt King Cobra in a webbed holster watched me drop the token into the slot and clack through the turnstile; watched me with a faint glimmer of undefined hope for a diversion from sore arches and atrophied reflexes. He and his fellows were highly visible at all the stations where the monorail stopped, a built-in deterrent to the class of passenger who travels with spray paint and a Buck knife. It's worked so far, but the People Mover is new and the flow of victims in the malls and arcades is still steady.

Thanks in part to the heavy security, the Greektown station and its counterparts are pretty things, all bright shining tile sporting artwork commissioned locally. The cars themselves, sleek and narrow and operated by computer, shuttle into and out of the stations at clockwork intervals, starting and stopping and working their sliding doors automatically. One was just heading out when I got there. I checked my watch: 11:25. I was a little early. While I was waiting, a chattering group of four men and three women, all in their twenties, came through the turnstile carrying shopping bags, and the cop lost interest in me temporarily. The next set of cars stopped and they climbed on board, still chattering. When the cars pulled out without me, I felt the cop's attention descend on me like a yoke of anvils.

A couple in their sixties joined me on the platform, the man leaning on an aluminum cane with three rubber feet. We waited in silence. After the next set of cars had stopped to let out three black youths in Mumford High School jackets and took off carrying the elderly couple, the cop approached me.

"Sir, the People Mover closes in fifteen minutes. Are you waiting for someone?"

He combed his graying hair sideways across his scalp and he had pale blue eyes in a pasty face with a livid strawberry mark on one side, going down inside his collar. One thumb rested on the black rubber butt of his King Cobra.

"I was," I said. "I guess he's not coming."

"Well, the next train's the last one tonight."

"Thanks."

He went back to his post without turning around.

We were the only people in the station when the last set of cars pulled in and the doors shunted open. I stepped aboard. Behind me the turnstile clacked, but by the time I turned around and sat on the bench facing that way, only the transit cop was in view of the windows. Whoever it was had boarded another car.

The doors slid shut and the cars started forward with a minimum of inertia, swaying a little from side to side. I was sharing the two benches with a black couple in their late teens, holding hands and gazing out the windows with that expression you can only afford to show before you turn twenty, and a carroty-haired, middle-aged man in tattered army fatigues holding a duffle in his lap with both hands. He was looking at the air between us and enjoying his last quarter-hour of climate control before leaning into the elements on his way to one of the all-night grind-houses uptown.

I stood up to admire the view, and immediately wished I hadn't. Gripping a steel handle, I seemed to be floating several stories above the pavement. I could see the lighted display windows of the shops below on Grand River and Michigan and the pools of pinkish light beneath the street lamps on Woodward and beyond them, wheeling away to the sky, the yellow and orange and blue and green and turquoise lights of a million windows, glittering like insects with hard shiny bodies on fresh tar. I was living in something I had tried hard to avoid dreaming in the first place.

A pre-recorded voice announced that Cadillac Center was coming up. The cars rolled to a gentle stop between glittering tiles arranged in a mosaic; the doors sighed open. The couple got off, still holding hands, and three people got on. The two women were together, wearing nurse's flare-bottomed white slacks and white orthopedic shoes showing under the hems of their dark coats. The third, a man, had on a gray suit and a light tan belted topcoat. He glanced at me without interest as he boarded, touched the nosepiece of his amber-tinted glasses, and grasped a handle farther down the car facing me.

We rode in silence past two stops. No one got on at either of them. The nurses sat together. One of them, ten or fifteen years younger than her companion, spent the time trying to talk her into trading shifts on Monday, but the other wasn't having any. The man in the tan coat gazed into the middle distance and swayed with the car, his right hand resting in his side pocket. The derelict in fatigues had his eyes closed and his mouth open.

The nurses got off at the Civic Center. Nobody boarded. As we swung along the river, flat black with the lights of Windsor scattered on the surface, I made my way over to the newcomer, cowboy style to avoid pitching onto one of the benches. His empty gaze didn't change as I approached. I stopped a few feet from him and took hold of one of the vertical poles that supported the roof with my left hand. I reached my right hand behind my back as if to scratch an itch and rested it on the grip of the .38.

We had the length of the car between us and the derelict, who was snoring now fit to start the screws that held the car together out of their holes. I kept my voice normal. "I said the Greektown station."

"Cadillac Center was closer," Sahara said. "I thought I made it clear yesterday you were fired. What's so important we have to meet aboard the mayor's electric train set at midnight?"

"It seemed an appropriate place." I leaned closer. "I know who killed Pingree. I know how it was done and why. Boy, you're a sap."

"Am I." No intonation. He could have gotten a job calling out the stations.

"I met Usher. Edgar Pym he calls himself here. I guess it's no worse than your Jerome Bosch. I can relate to all these literary and artistic allusions you fellows use to break up the monotony. Everyone has his little tricks: I crack wise, cops mess around with the Bill of Rights, politicians mess around,

158

period. It gets us all in trouble sometimes, but without it living is just surviving. Usher told me about the list of field agents you stole. He says he's under orders not to negotiate."

"If he weren't, it wouldn't have been him they sent. Naturally I don't know anything about a list."

"Naturally. Just like you didn't know that those downtown locations on Pingree's sheet were stops for the People Mover, and had no idea why anyone would ride around in a complete circle and get off where he got on. Or where she got on," I corrected.

The cars stopped at the Renaissance Center. The doors beside us opened. No one entered. They closed. We resumed moving.

Sahara said, "She."

"She as in her. Her as in the woman in the case. You said yourself they got caught up in these things."

"You mean Catherine?"

"Now you're playing stupid. I thought invisibility was your trick."

His amber gaze didn't change. "You couldn't take your hooks off it, could you? Even when I gave you an out. That was for your benefit, Walker. I could have let you fall through the same hole as Pingree."

"Stop rewriting your part. You're a sap, not a hero. You cut me loose because I was too close to finding out what you'd just discovered for yourself."

"National security is a factor in everything I—"

"Park that. You can't be a rogue agent and walk the party line at the same time. You just didn't want the whole world to find out that Bill Sahara, the gray ghost, double-oh-wonderful, got himself set up by a woman, and a nonprofessional at that. That's the problem with being a pro and working with and against other pros: You can't predict what an amateur's going to do. That wild card throws off every hand."

"It works both ways," he said, and kicked me in the chest with both feet.

I wasn't prepared for it. I'd been watching the pocket with his hand in it, waiting for the shape to change. Instead he put all his weight on the hand gripping the steel handle over his head and reared back with both feet and kicked out like a mule. That made me a sap, too. Despite what I knew about him, his bland businessman's disguise had made me forget for a moment that he would be in top condition and that a gun was only one of the many ways he could kill. I had reacted quickly to the sudden movement, leaning back as I slid the revolver from my belt holster, and that saved me from having my chest caved in, but my lungs emptied with a woof and I fell over on my back, landing hard on my gun arm and driving all the feeling out of my fingers. I didn't even know if I was still holding the weapon.

"Freeze!"

Well, some of them still say it, in spite of the bad rap it's gotten from television, and just then it sounded as sweet as anything I'd ever heard, because Sahara's hand was out of his pocket now and I was looking up the inside of the suppressor screwed to the barrel of his Walther GSP, a twin of the automatic I'd taken away from his man Wessell. The shout, coming from the far end of the car, rattled him, but he didn't take his eyes or the gun off me: SOP in a situation like that is to shoot your primary target and deal with the third party afterward. But the split second the shout brought me was enough to let me bring round the .38, which was still in my hand after all. The fact that I'd need a bulldozer to pull the trigger in my present condition was immaterial. It was one too many guns for him and he froze.

I was sitting up on the floor now with my shoulder against the vertical pole I'd been holding before. Out of the corner of my eye I could see the tramp in fatigues standing with his legs spread in the aisle, a revolver thrust out in front of him in both hands. "Drop it!" he shouted, adding another sterling phrase to the lexicon. "Now!"

I put an oar in. "Bill Sahara, meet Officer Mark Ashley of the East Detroit Police Department, Criminal Investigation Division. I think the wardrobe's his."

"Burack," he corrected. "Ashley couldn't make it. Drop the piece or I'll blow you into the next car!"

160

He was getting better, but I didn't have time to congratulate him. In the excitement, I'd missed the announcement that we were heading into the Grand Circus station. The car slowed and stopped. The doors opened at Sahara's elbow and a woman in a fur coat stepped off the platform. Sahara hurled an arm across her throat, drew her against him, and rammed the suppressor under her chin. She had another chin to spare, and they both began to quiver. "Your turn, the pair of you," he said. "I don't have to tell you what happens if you don't."

A transit cop built along the lines of his counterpart in Trappers Alley, but with more hair and less birthmark, drew his Colt. Sahara changed his angle a notch to bring him into his field of vision. "You, too, brother. Let me hear them drop."

It seemed longer than it was; the doors don't stay open beyond thirty seconds. We were like that for a while, painted there like the artwork on the tiles, and then there was a flash of movement outside the windows and a noise that for an instant I thought was the report of the suppressed automatic, only it was too dull for that. Sahara arched his back, loosening his grip, and the woman ducked out from under with admirable reflexes and ran off kiyoodling toward the station exit, which was her earned right. Meanwhile Sahara's legs did a slow fold and he slid down the pole at his back for a foot or so before sagging forward to his knees and then, ostrichlike, onto his face. The left bow of his eyeglasses came away from his ear. It all took probably less than ten seconds. Enough time anyway for Papa Frank Usher, wearing the same cut-rate sport coat and golf greens he'd had on when I met him, to take another step and swing his stick a second time, a short brutal expert arc. This time the noise was more emphatic. A black stream of the fluid the brain floats in joined the puddle of red on the floor from the first blow.

The doors tried to close, encountered Sahara's gun arm lying across the threshold, and reversed directions, sending a silent signal to the central computer to shut down the entire system. As a symbol it was pretty poetry.

161

26

THERE WERE PLENTY OF COPS AROUND AFTER THAT. A GANG
of uniforms from the Detroit Tactical Mobile Unit arrived
minutes after the first officers on the scene and set up saw-
horses to keep the Saturday night crowds at bay, followed
closely by a pair of plainclothes detectives I knew slightly
from 1300 Beaubien, Detroit Police Headquarters, who split
us up for questioning. Officer Burack showed his East Detroit
badge and credentials, but Usher stole his thunder with the
impressive-looking CIA card in its neat leather folder and
declined to provide any answers on the scene. He was as
calm as a fence rail. The rest of us were still into the prelim-
inaries when the detectives elected to take us down to 1300
and drop us in the inspector's lap.

One more thing before we leave the Grand Circus station.

While the transit cop was busy holding back citizens before reinforcements arrived, I directed Burack's attention
away from Usher while he went through Sahara's pockets.
Later, amid the orderly confusion of cops at work, I got
Usher into a corner.

"Did he have it on him?"

He nodded. "Also a pair of airline tickets one way to
Panama, today's date. I left those. Not the best place to hide
from the Company, but from there he could have caught a

boat or a plane to anywhere. Both tickets were in the name of Henry Deimling. Recognize it?''

"No, but I bet if you go back far enough you'll find Henry's obituary. Died in infancy. You know that dodge.''

"First week of training." He got out a cigar and slid it along his lower lip, moistening the end. "Thanks for the diversion.''

"You didn't have to hit him twice.''

"Sure I did. Just like I had to ride in the next car. He might have recognized me. Anyone ever tell you you're not an easy man to follow?''

"I figured you'd keep up.''

He looked at his cigar. "Find out what you needed to know?''

"Only what I suspected going in. Sahara didn't kill Pingree. He barely knew Pingree existed.''

"He'd have killed you, though. You and Burack and the woman and the rent-a-cop would've been dead thirty seconds after you dropped your guns. I've seen it before. When a field man of Sahara's classification slips the harness he turns into a natural disaster.''

"That's what I was thinking.''

"What would you have done if I hadn't come along?''

"Shot him.''

"He'd still have killed the woman. He had trained reflexes.''

"That's why I'm glad you came along.''

"It's my job, son.''

"Just for the record, I think your job stinks.''

"It don't smell any prettier from my side." He produced an orange plastic throwaway lighter, looked around, spotted the NO SMOKING sign and put it away, smiling faintly behind his moustache; the rules you keep, the rules you break. "I know you don't like what I stand for, son. I didn't like what that little storm trooper Strendle stood for either. When you're going down for the third time and a hand reaches out over the side of the boat you don't look at it too close." He put his out, tentatively.

This time I took it.

* * *

I was drinking a cup of paint thinner at a table in one of the interrogation rooms downtown when John Alderdyce came in. We hadn't seen each other in months, and the change threw me. He had lost some more hair, throwing the bones of his coarse African face into even greater relief. Naturally bulky, he had in the months of physical inactivity behind an inspector's desk put on at least thirty pounds. Soon he would be fat. He walked like a fat man and his camel's-hair jacket, fashioned as always from the best material, was cut like a tent. He made his way around the table and dropped heavily into the only other chair, sitting with his knees spread to make room for a belly he didn't have yet.

"How's your arm?'" he asked.

I rubbed it. "I banged the elbow when I fell. My fingertips are still numb, but I don't have any piano recitals coming up for a while."

"I read your statement. It doesn't say why you brought along an East Detroit officer without notifying Detroit."

"It was their case. Pingree was killed in East Detroit. Anyway I didn't bring him along. I called up there and they sent down Burack. I was told he'd be wearing the homeless look."

"He was out of his jurisdiction. I don't have to tell you what you're out of."

"Take that up with his chief. Maybe they were afraid you'd fill the place with uniforms and scare Sahara off. It isn't as if no Detroit cop ever made a bust up there without telling the locals what he was about."

"Cops can get away with it, sometimes. Don't forget it's always open season on private heat." He fished a half-empty pack of Chesterfields out of his shirt pocket and played with it, propping his elbows on the table. He'd been quitting smoking almost as long as he'd been smoking. "Why'd Sahara poison Pingree? Your statement wasn't clear on that."

"He didn't."

"Then maybe you can tell me why Sahara's taking up morgue space here."

164

"What did Usher tell you?"

"Usher?"

"Here he's Pym, sorry. Spies." I shrugged.

"He didn't tell me anything. We're all just kind of sitting around waiting for Washington to open shop so he can get orders. I thought maybe you'd help kill some time."

"It's goofy," I said. "I wouldn't buy a ticket if someone described it to me. I think Sahara agreed to meet me so he could clean house before he left the country. I think he had that in his mind from the start, once I'd established a new identity for him and made all the arrangements. I would have been the only thing to link him to his new life and he couldn't afford to leave me in a talking condition. That business with Gail Hope and the quarter million proved I was honest, but he'd seen honest men broken when it was in someone's interest to break them. He'd probably broken his share.

"Some of it was pride; an unaffordable luxury when your greatest goal in life is to be inconspicuous. He was a man who was supposed to know all the angles, he was being taken for a ride on a little death like Pingree's, and I knew about it and was rubbing his nose in it. I admit I was shoving him pretty hard. He went over quicker than I expected. Usher happening along when he did made things a little less messy."

"Usher—Pym, whatever—he had the contract on Sahara, that it?"

"So I gathered. The Company gets sore when you quit without two weeks' notice." I had left all mention of the list of agents out of my statement. It had seemed like enough without the list.

"So who killed Pingree?"

"Why ask, John? That's East Detroit's wagon."

Someone knocked. He let whoever it was knock again, looking at me. Finally he got up and went to the door. There was a whispered conversation and Alderdyce left the room. A few minutes later he came back and stood by the table.

165

"You must have voted right in the last election, Walker. You know the way out."

I didn't move. "Washington get back to you?"

"They called the commissioner, got him out of bed. He called me. I never knew what I was missing when I was just a lieutenant. You get your ass chewed out by a whole different class of people up here."

"Sorry, John. If there was any other way to play it."

"My ass can stand a little chewing. God knows it's big enough these days. I'm still a peace officer, even if I do spend most of my time stapling crime statistics together. I like to think I'm making a difference. Only just about the time I think I'm doing that, along comes a piecework sleuth and a government spook to start dropping bodies in my lap, as if the four hundred others that got there ahead of it since January weren't enough. Then as soon as I finish with my little broom and dustpan, someone whose window looks out on the Capitol Building instead of an airshaft snatches it away. Do me a favor and take it down the street. I've got a press statement to write and only two hours to make it sound like I didn't just get back from Oz."

I rose. "I wasn't going to mention the weight gain. You ought to take up handball."

He went out, leaving the door open.

Outside 1300 the sky behind Windsor was getting rosy. The freezing rain had left a knobby crust on the sidewalks and pavement. A salt truck grumbled around the corner on Jefferson. As the light in the east intensified, it prismed through the hoarfrost on the street lamps and on the concrete supports of the People Mover, as quiet now as bones in a museum; needling the downtown area in rainbow colors. The colors reminded me of where I wanted to go from there.

The cops had picked me up in a blue-and-white and turned me out without a ride, same as always. On Brush, a Checker cab let off a fare who smelled too freshly of liquor as I stepped past him to have come from anywhere but an after-hours joint. I sank into a black leather seat permeated with tobacco

166

to its springs and closed my eyes. The driver's "Where to?" woke me up.

"The Club Canaveral."

27

I PAID THE DRIVER, A DARK-SKINNED ARAB WHO HELD MY bill between his teeth while he made change from a White Owl cigar box in his lap. "You sure I can't take you someplace else, mister?" he said. "The place looks closed."

"Thanks. I'm sure."

As he rolled off, tires spinning a little on the slick asphalt, I went down the alley next to the building and stopped in front of the brown fire door. Dead-bolt locks are only effective if your intruder doesn't know how to pick the oldest, simplest Yale in existence. I made some scratches and barked a knuckle hard enough to start it bleeding and was inside in three minutes.

In the orange light of an exit sign I navigated my way past the rest rooms and across the dance floor, echoing like an aircraft hanger, to the office. Some of the dawn was coming in under the shades on the windows.

This lock was an ordinary spring latch and I slipped it in two seconds with one of the celluloid compartments from my wallet. There being no window in the office, I snapped on the ceiling light. The room was anonymous but for the Impressionist street scene hanging behind the desk, a nononsense place of business in contrast to the splashed pastels and camp posters in the nightclub itself. The air smelled faintly of something I recognized as Gail Hope's perfume.

Daughter Evelyn watched me wandering the room from her Lucite stand on the black steel desk.

I found it in the only place it could have been hidden, a wooden two-drawer file cabinet supporting a yellow fern in a hand-thrown clay pot. The typewriter was a Royal, one of the old gray manuals with rounded edges like a tank's. I lifted it and carried it over to the desk, where it went like hell with the computer terminal on the nearby stand. I sat down and opened and closed desk drawers until I found some stationery and cranked a sheet into the machine. When I was through typing I tore out the sheet and compared it with a paper I took from my pocket. I'd typed the names of as many of the People Mover's downtown stations as I could remember. The Royal's lower-case *w* had a piece broken off and the *a* was slightly out of line. The sheet from Herbert S. Pingree's effects showed the same flaws. The ribbon needed changing.

I folded both sheets and put them in my pocket. Then I made two telephone calls. When that was done I fingered out my cigarette pack, but it was empty. I crumpled it and threw it into the wastebasket. My mouth tasted like cotton filters anyway.

I must have dozed. I came forward in the chair when the fire door boomed shut. Footsteps clicked across the dance floor. The doorknob turned and she came in.

No denim shirt and blue jeans this time. No slinky gown and stilts either. She'd put on a plaid caped overcoat with Madame Butterfly sleeves and a pair of black patent-leather pumps with two-inch heels. With her light brown hair pinned up and makeup on she looked taller, but she would always give the impression of a little girl playing dress-up. She wasn't carrying a purse.

"I could have you arrested for breaking and entering," she said.

"They'd just throw me back out in the street. I wore out my welcome there an hour ago."

"All right, you called and I'm here. I said I was sorry about the other thing. Sahara didn't give me any choice."

"Sahara's dead."

She wasn't quick enough to cover it. She was a better actress than anyone had given her credit for, but the hour was early and I'd sprung it on her. For an instant there it was Christmas. Then she sobered. "What happened?"

"I happened. Usher happened. You happened. Not in that order." I told her about it. When I mentioned the People Mover I was watching her closely but this time she'd had a chance to prepare. I didn't get anything out of it.

"I'm not sorry," she said. "He used me. I might as well have been working for the studios. I'm only surprised that he waited to quit. I always thought he loved his job, the rotten bastard."

"When you burn out you burn out. He had two tickets to Central America in his pocket. One of them was for you, wasn't it?"

She overplayed it that time. Well, it had been years since the cameras had rolled. "Uh-huh, yeah. I'd sooner go off with Hitler."

"I believe you. But that's not what you told Sahara. How long had you been sleeping with him? Don't answer, it doesn't matter. Long enough anyway to convince a man whose business is to trust no one to take you into his confidence. Long before I entered the picture. No wonder he was amused when I said my helping him out of his job would get you out of his vest pocket. Did you laugh about it late that night in bed?"

"You're as sick as he was if you think that."

"Only a lover could have gotten him to confide as much as he did. He told you he was quitting, about the list of undercover agents he'd swiped, either to insure his safety or to extort some case dough out of Uncle Sam. About the people who would enter their own bids. Only a lover—or an actress who could pose as one." I patted the machine on the desk. "You haven't asked me why the typewriter isn't in the file cabinet where it belongs."

"It's a little early in the morning to worry about typewriters, especially with a crazy man in the room."

170

"Now you're chewing the scenery, Gail. Or do you prefer Vadya?"

She lost a little color when I mentioned the part she played in *V-8 Vampires*. Sarah Bernhardt couldn't control that. No reaction otherwise. I let it slide for now and put the two typewritten sheets on the desk.

"They match, of course," I said. "You couldn't forge Pingree's hand, but you should have gotten rid of the typewriter. Maybe you didn't think anyone would get this far. The People Mover stations were what you wanted them to notice. Since Sahara wouldn't just ride around aimlessly day after day, it suggested he was meeting someone. Why? To collect bids on that hot list of agents."

I heard a noise in the nightclub. She had left the door open a crack when she came in. I went on. "I can only guess at the amount of homework it took to find an investigator like Pingree. Maybe not so much; every business has its misfits. In any case he was the ultimate pigeon. Did you come to him as Gail Hope, fading movie queen, or as a distraught housewife?"

"It's your story," she said.

"I like distraught housewife. He was young enough not to have seen any of your pictures. He was also a trusting soul, and business was just bad enough to keep him from checking your scenario, if he even knew how. You knew all about Catherine. She even looks like the Other Woman. You came to Pingree, or more likely you met him somewhere to avoid his nosy neighbors, cried a little into a handkerchief like you did in *Beach Blowout*, told him you suspected Catherine of having an affair with your husband, and gave him a lot of money to follow her around. You asked him to keep the job off the books. He agreed, and made good on his agreement. I have to like him for that, harebrained as it was. Men who come through on their promises are rare and getting rarer. You counted on that. There must be no evidence to suggest you ever made contact."

I heard nothing more from the direction of the nightclub.

I hadn't expected to hear anything to begin with. I'd been in the land of the professionals on this one from the start.

"Naturally, Catherine spotted the tail," I said. "Pingree was as conspicuous as Sahara was invisible. She wouldn't go to her husband, because she'd suspect her husband of hiring him in the first place. She'd come to me, being a detective and being in town, but mostly being her ex-husband. That made me a valuable witness. I knew about Pingree, had even spoken with him. Sahara would have told you that. By now he was telling you everything. No wonder he kicked me when I called him a sap. It was easier than kicking himself.

"Maybe my talking to Pingree forced your hand. Even he was starting to smell a Hollywood rat and considered taking me into his confidence. No matter. It was a good time to move." I tapped the typewritten itinerary. "You'd already given him this, because he'd had time to run off a copy and put it in the safe deposit box where he kept copies of all his records. He was definitely suspicious or he wouldn't have gone to so much trouble to hide the originals in the toilet on his floor. I'm not clear yet on what story you told him when you gave him the paper. Planting it on him after he was dead might not have worked. Maybe you knew about the bank box and thought someone would be suspicious if there weren't a copy of the itinerary in it. It had to convince some people for whom suspicion is a way of life."

"You're doing a lot of talking for someone who isn't saying anything." As she spoke she moved away from the door. The action might have been unconscious.

"Indulge me. I'm a lonely man. Pingree was crucial, maybe for the only time in his life. If the people who were watching Sahara—the people being Frank Usher, Edgar Pym, Papa, whatever Death is calling itself this season—if they were to buy the premise that Sahara was getting set to peddle that list and sign the death warrant for dozens of deep-cover agents placed at no small expense in key areas across the country, you needed a corpse to put the point across. This is where Gail Hope, former celluloid beach bunny and present Detroit bistro owner, trades petty intrigue for evil genius.

"A dead private investigator with evidence of treason is hard to ignore. The conclusion was inevitable: dick catches spy with his hand in the till, dick blackmails spy, spy kills dick. Using cyanide was a neat touch. A little showy, a little Technicolor and Cinemascope, but so much more in character for an egotistical snuff artist like Sahara than just a bullet. A corpse and evidence suggesting contact with people who buy government secrets. The courts would need more to convict. Usher wouldn't." I was watching her closely. "You must have hated Sahara's guts and the box they came in."

"I did. Like I said, he used me." She was standing clear of the door now, directly under the ceiling light. Hairline cracks showed in her make-up, like fissures in an ancient painting. "He would have gone on using me, all because I was young and stupid enough once to believe him when he said I could make the world a better place by getting my Sam to become a stooge for the Feds." She leaned forward. "But like *you* said, the courts would need more to prove anything. If that piece of paper is all you've got . . ."

"It was gaping at me all along, but I'm slow sometimes. You might say someone had to draw me a picture. A moving picture. I screened *V-8 Vampires* last night."

"That piece of crap."

"I agree. The aging scene was the best thing in it. You make a convincing old lady. That's when I remembered something Sergeant Trilby had told me, about the building cleaning crew and the scrubwoman on Pingree's floor the morning he was killed." I paused. "You did your own make-up in *Vampires*, didn't you?"

She laughed. It wasn't her Malibu giggle.

"I read about the poisoning in the papers," she said. "Pingree's neighbor heard a man's voice through the wall. Not a woman's."

"I already said you were no petty intriguer. You knew better than to say anything out loud in a crackerbox like that. Of course you had help. You couldn't be sure he'd take the poison when you offered it, and small as he was you'd be no

173

match for him if you tried to force it down his throat. There was a window washer on that floor as well."

"There's one here, too."

The new voice was run-of-the-mill, without a regional accent. You could hear it through a wall and not be able to identify it later. It belonged to a young man in a blue suit who came through the door with a gun in his hand, an L-frame Smith & Wesson nine-millimeter automatic with twice the penetrating power of my old Police Special. His hair was short and dark blond and he had a short nose and a long upper lip and dark eyes with long Mediterranean lashes against very fair skin. He was well-proportioned and didn't look as big as he actually was; his hand swallowed much of the large pistol. I looked at him a long time before I remembered where I'd seen him last, guarding the door to the hospital room where Sam Lucy lay plugged into an artificial life-support system.

28

"WHO'S GUARDING LUCY?" I ASKED. "OR DID YOU FINALLY decide that's like locking an empty safe?"

The big man said, "He died last night. Never regained consciousness. Gail was there."

"So it's Gail, is it?" I looked at her. "You don't let any grass grow."

"I did most of my scenes in one take." She stepped out from under the direct light. "You guess pretty good. Some of the details are wrong. I told Pingree that Catherine was my brother's wife and that I thought she was stepping out on him, not that she was having an affair with my husband. I also told him I'd tried following her myself, and that's when I gave him the itinerary. It's genuine, by the way. I arranged those appointments and I kept them."

"Ah."

"Bill was so charged over his precious list he insisted on telling me the names of all the people who would pay millions for it. You'd be surprised how many of them operate in this area; you'd be surprised how many of them are listed. What's so funny?"

I stopped grinning. "You had my sympathy for a while there. Not for Pingree, but for wanting to nail Sahara. It's a respectable aspiration, revenge. It feels too good in practice

175

to be as bad as the ministers say. It isn't enough for some people, though. Some people have to make it pay."

"It didn't start out like that. I set up the first meetings aboard the People Mover to lay down a background. If the itinerary wasn't enough to hand Sahara, I could always claim I was representing his interests. But when I told them what he had and how it was obtained, the figures they mentioned made my toes curl. Yes, I had to make it pay. Why not? I earned every cent."

"How were you planning to deliver?"

"If I couldn't get the list away from Sahara, I'd have faked something when the time came. Spies are dull. They think everyone else is as dull as they are. They'd have met me more than halfway."

"Everyone else did," I said. "Pingree may have been a goat, but it was a big herd."

"Everything I am I owe to men."

Her lips didn't appear to move as she said it. It was as if I were looking at one of her posters and the words were in my head.

"So what happens now? I should tell you I'm not thirsty."

She laughed again. "I wouldn't dream of using cyanide a second time. You broke into this building, into my office. What do you think's going to happen?"

"I'm disappointed. Any of the hacks who wrote your stuff in the old days could have come up with a more original plot."

"That's the thing about clichés. They work." She smoothed the skirt of her coat. "Dennis is my new chief of security—bouncer to you. I don't even have to be here for this." She turned toward the door.

Big Dennis gestured with the automatic. "Bring 'em up."

I didn't move. "Haven't you been listening?"

"Up." He flicked back the hammer.

My revolver, which I'd been holding inside the kneehole of the desk, jumped in my hand. There's only one sure target at that angle. The bullet punched a hole through the modesty panel and plowed into his groin. He made an indescribable noise and lost all interest in his weapon.

He was still standing, though, when Gail Hope sent me a look over her shoulder that reminded me of her aging, decomposing vampire with the flesh peeling away from its skull and broke into a run. I raised the Smith & Wesson and took aim at her back. Not a woman's back, not Gail Hope's back. Not even a back. A target.

I didn't fire. If I had, the bullet might have passed through her and struck Sergeant Trilby. He threw both arms around her, a reflex gesture to keep his balance when she ran into him, and hung on. His service pistol was in his right hand. There was a struggle, but he held her until one of the uniforms he'd brought with him could lend some muscle. There were three of them. Two wore the blue with brown trim of the Detroit Police Department. Inspector Alderdyce would approve of that.

Dennis chose that moment to fall. His blue serge pants were drenched with blood and urine when he toppled forward from the waist and disappeared below the edge of the desk. He groaned when he hit the floor and went on groaning.

By this time I'd placed my gun on the desk in plain sight and folded my hands on top of my head. The two officers not involved with handcuffing Gail Hope had taken up positions on both sides of the door with their sidearms out in the two-handed stance. One of them was a large woman in her early thirties with her hair tucked up under her cap. I found out later her name was Heidi.

"It's okay," Trilby said. "He's a friendly."

The guns came down and my hands with them. Gail was breathing heavily with her wrists linked behind her back, looking at no one, saying nothing. Something about her had crumpled in. She looked like a little old lady, although she was barely in her forties. I had seen her do it before but that had been in a movie, and there had been special effects involved.

Trilby, wearing his three-button suit and car coat, hol-

177

stered his revolver under his arm. I asked him how much he had heard.

"Enough to charge. Maybe enough to convict, with that typewriter. Who's this?" He did something with his foot. Dennis' automatic scraped across the floor and bumped into a wall.

"He used to throw himself in front of bullets for Sam Lucy."

"Looks like he was good at it. That phone work?"

"I used it to call you."

He dialed 911 and ordered an EMS unit. Hanging up, he looked at his watch. "Twenty-seven hours short of the deadline. Not too shabby."

"I've cut it closer," I said.

"What makes all this easier than just tipping me the whole shebang in the first place?"

I rubbed my eyes. They were burning and I realized I'd been up all night. "A long time ago I represented a client who stood to lose his life if certain information reached certain people. A very long time ago: all the way back yesterday. Business isn't so good I can afford to help kill off customers. You know part of it, if your man Burack has filed his report."

"I read it. You bought yourself some slack when you invited us in on that show downtown. That's all you bought. We're not in business to provide backup for you. Next time—no, there won't be a next time. Keep it out of East Detroit."

"Funny, that's what an inspector told me a little while ago. Only he said keep it out of Detroit."

"Your circle's getting tight, Walker. Maybe you ought to consider changing your methods."

"I considered it," I said.

"And?"

"Nah."

I left just behind the ambulance. The paramedics thought they could help Dennis hang on to the cup of blood he had left until they got to Detroit General, after which he was somebody else's headache. I went home to sleep, gave up on that after an hour, got up and called the hospital. A nurse told me the emergency shooting case they had taken in that morning was still in the operating room. I took a shower, shaved, dressed, rode in a cab to the lot where I'd parked my car the night before and drove up to East Detroit to dictate the complete statement I'd promised Trilby. The tape recorder took it all down without scowling. Afterward I ate a late breakfast at the Black Bull. When I caught myself falling face first into my eggs I paid the tab and went back home and slept sixteen hours straight. I dreamed not at all.

I was in the office at seven o'clock Monday morning. The mail wasn't in yet and my answering service wouldn't report for another hour, so I started a fresh pack of Winstons and called Detroit General. Dennis Arguella was critical but stable after a four-hour operation to remove a bullet and graft a new piece onto his femoral artery. After a few games of Solitaire the mailman whistled his way into the outer office and I watched two bills, a contest circular, and a picture postcard slither through the brass slot. When my curiosity overcame my inertia I got up and went over and picked up the mail. The postcard was an advertisement from a travel agency in Redford.

I sat down awhile, stood at the window awhile, sat down again and called my service. There were no messages. I tried to interest the girl in conversation. She was polite. She told me good-bye before she hung up in my face.

I was wired. I had enough energy for two detectives and not a kidnapped heiress or a missing set of crown jewels in sight. I thought about a vacation. What I had in savings ought to get me as far as the Ohio border if I didn't mind pushing my car back. When the telephone finally rang I hoped it was the post office saying a check had come for me express, would I come down and sign for it? It wasn't. It was Albert Schindler, informing me he'd found the very car I was looking for and that it would run me a thousand on top of the five hundred I'd given him. It took me a moment to remember why I'd wanted the car in the first place. I told him that case had gone sour. He said something in German and hung up without saying good-bye.

The buzzer sounded in the outer office as I was replacing the receiver. "Enter, friend."

Catherine had on her silver fox coat over a black shift and black pumps. I stood up.

"The funeral's today," she said without greeting. "I thought I might as well get it over with."

"I didn't want it that way."

"Just don't tell me you're sorry." She sat down and shrugged out of the coat. Her arms were bare. I couldn't remember if funeral etiquette covered that, but it wouldn't have mattered to her. The plain black showed off her athletic figure. "The office hasn't changed. Same old dump."

I sat. "I like it."

It sounded defensive. She raised her eyebrows but didn't comment. "I read about what happened. What the police say happened. I mean with the Hope woman. I couldn't make sense out of it."

"You're not supposed to. The blanket's on. Have you heard from Pym?"

"He stood me up Saturday night. When I tried to call his apartment I got a recording saying the number was no longer in service. The building superintendent said he'd moved out, no forwarding, with eight months to go on a year's lease. Would you know anything about it?"

There'd been no mention of Usher under any name in the news reports of the People Mover shooting. William Sahara was identified as a despondent civil servant whom police had slain in a hostage situation. No connection was made with the Pingree murder or the arrest the next morning of former movie beach goddess Gail Hope; the media were still trying to sort out that one. "I told you why Pym was here," I said. "Sahara's dead, he's gone. What else do you need?"

She was going to fight me over it. I saw that, and I saw when she wasn't.

"I just wish I knew where you figured in this," she said. "I just wish I knew that."

"That's the first thing you and I ever had in common."

She blew out some air. "Well, I'm back where I started. Only this time I'm a widow."

"Any plans?"

"Get a job, I suppose. The son of a bitch didn't have any insurance."

"Spies are bum risks."

"So are detectives. I sure know how to pick 'em." She got up and put on her coat. "Did you have breakfast?"

"Are you inviting me?"

"Don't read anything into it."

I'd been playing with the picture postcard, sliding it around the blotter on its slick surface with the eraser end of a pencil. I flipped it over, looked at the picture, yellow sand and creaming surf. Then I chucked it into the wastebasket and went for my coat and hat.

"Let's not get married this time," I said.

ABOUT THE AUTHOR

Since the appearance of his first novel in 1976, Loren D. Estleman has written more than two dozen books. He has received the Western Writers of America Spur Award twice and the Private Eye Writers of America Shamus Award three times. Estleman has also been nominated for the American Book Award and the Pulitzer Prize. He is a veteran police-court journalist and a native Detroiter who now lives in Whitmore Lake, Michigan, with his wife, Carole Ashley.